Falling Up

or

How to Get to Proxima Centauri.

By Mike McCulloch

To Boksun

Chapter 1. Maati (The name of the person whose point of view it is). Foot repair in the outer Sol system (Chapter title).

When Saturn sets behind its moon Enceladus, Morley the robot and I often aim our digiscope at the small pin-prick of Terra in the constellation Tadpole. From way out here, Terra and Venus are celestial sisters, both white, Venus because of its clouds, Terra because of its ice. Only the double belt of green around Terra's equator shows that some life survived the Great Crustal Shift, an event in which Terra's solid crust rotated on top of the liquid mantle (see my sketch below) causing abrupt changes in climate all over the globe.

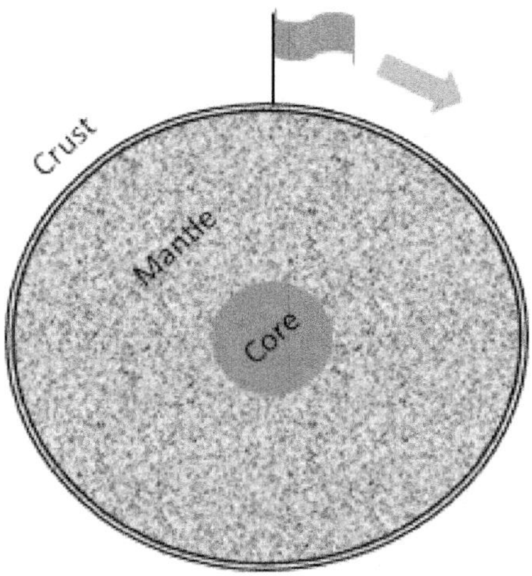

We also survived, a mining colony orbiting Saturn's moon Enceladus of cold-adapted Inuit miners, and hard-working

Amish farmers who came here following their desire to be separate from the world.

My name is Maati Jaspersen: female, small, red haired. I specialise in hydroponics, which is the growing of food without soil - essential in our soil-less metal home, and I also love robots, for which I have suffered much abuse.

There are also some small groups of Russians, Chinese and Europeans who made a rebel Trek from Terra about 40 years ago, but the third main ethnic group around our colonies, in my opinion, are the robots. Morley, for example, the sweetie, came to the colonies with the exodus from Terra. Over the years so many defective bits of him have been replaced that he is physically a new robot many times over, barring his neural patterns. He is one of the old kind. They could build robots in the days before the Big Shift destroyed most industry, but he is 40 years old and, just like a human of that age, is just beginning to break up a little.

His problem on this particular day was that his inertial floaters were on the fritz with the result that the poor dustbin, every so often, lurched comically sideways into walls, so after our brief look at distant Terra, I detached his foot and a began to clean it. Deprived of motion he chirped away happily, in his idiosyncratic pigeon English. My sister stormed into the lab when I was about to reattach his right foot and berated me in Inuit, which I translate:

“There you are! What the hell are you doing here? It’s a free day, y’know!”
“I’m looking after Morley.”
“Oh bosh. Looks like you’re working!”
“Someone has to keep things in order. We don’t want chaos.”
“Yes we do. It’s fun.”
“Look, let me just switch his poor feet back on...”
“Leave it to friggin’ Dad. He’s supposed to do that.”

Studiously ignoring her, I switched Morley’s pods on. Immediately he rose up into the air, and hovered facing me performing his favourite joke, which is it to hover about five degrees off horizontal, just enough to be subliminally confusing to humans. I gamely tilted my head slightly in the same skew and he went into a silicon orgasm of delight at this and began flying in circles - his way of laughing. I grinned ecstatically at my sister, but she just shook her head.

“You’re more attached to robots than people! It’s not natural.”
“Robots are people!”
“You’re hopeless. Do you want to have some real fun?”
“Like what?”
“I’ve just seen the seaweed farm - it’s crawling with friggin’ robots.”

Morley bobbed close to my head, and spoke in his pigeon English.

“Morley knows weed in A4 ready. He help pick, but foot kaput!”

My sister looked at Morley in irritation. I can never understand her attitude towards robots. She seemed to think they were less than human. For me, carbon, silicon, what's the difference? So long as you have a sense of humour, and Morley could reduce even the Amish to ridiculous giggling.

"Oh stop yabb'ring to the floating brick there... Let's go and get some!"
"Before we go, do you want to see Terra through the telescope?"
"No. Planetful of frozen losers, if you ask me."
"I'd like to go someday..."
"What for? Must still be like hell down there... Now, how about that seaweed?"

Chapter 2. Dork Stratoe. A Little Horizon Drive.

I was born shortly after the Big Shift into a European refugee settlement in the cooler highlands of Ethiopia and like many at this time I was named after one of the thousands of species extinct beneath the ice sheets. I might have hoped to be named after something noble like "Eagle", but at that time, just after a period of extreme hunger and stress, frugal animals were respected and so my parents chose Dormouse. Not the most masculine of names, but there you go. People have commented on its aptness: I fall asleep a lot, and when not sleeping, I daydream. At school, Dormouse became contracted to Dork, which was a comment on my studious and offbeat nature. Eventually I came to like the name.

I was an only child (the law still limits families to one child since we are still a billion people crammed into the tropics) and my parents, who were the best people you could imagine, died in the epidemics that raged through crowded humanity when I was young. A dying society is no place for dreams, nevertheless, I've had a waking dream since childhood of freeing humanity from the Solar System by developing antigravity and hyperspace travel. So, of course, I studied physics in New Cambridge, which is actually located in a forested place formally called Bahir Dar in Ethiopia, and during my PhD I worked on a controversial method of modifying inertia to generate antigravity, based on theoretical work from before the Big Shift.

Then, of course, the world government forbade non-military space travel and the whole subject was closed down. So, for ten years I have been working at the United Nations Department for Monitoring the Use of Space (UNMUS). I know and love inertial and antigravity theory, and space in general, but this negative line of work is the only way I can apply it, since real research is banned.

After work I can often be found, as today, gazing out the window into the darkening evening from the 14th floor of a tower block at the torrential rain and making mental calculations. In the distance the view is of hundreds of other similar blocks rising out of the steaming Ethiopian highland jungle, lit up intermittently with lightning strikes: our main source of energy. On this particular day I was making the final adjustments to the illegal inertial physics experiment I had been refining for five years.

Inertia of course is that behaviour by which everyday object that do not feel friction, such as bowling balls travel in straight lines. Why? It had been proved, before the Big Shift that this is caused by curious mix of relativity and quantum mechanics. Whenever objects accelerate they see a radiation called Unruh radiation, that non-accelerating objects next to them do not see. This radiation forms a thermal bath around the objects. I have drawn a schematic below. The object is shown by the black arrow, and the Unruh radiation is shown by the lighter areas. Also, from relativity, we can say that the object in its acceleration sees an information horizon behind it since light cannot catch up to it from behind that horizon. See the black rectangle. This horizon damps the radiation behind the object, see the darker grey area, just as a seawall damps waves near to it, so more Unruh radiation pushes on the object from in front of it than from behind and that pushes the object back against its initial acceleration. So that is where the phenomenon of inertia comes from.

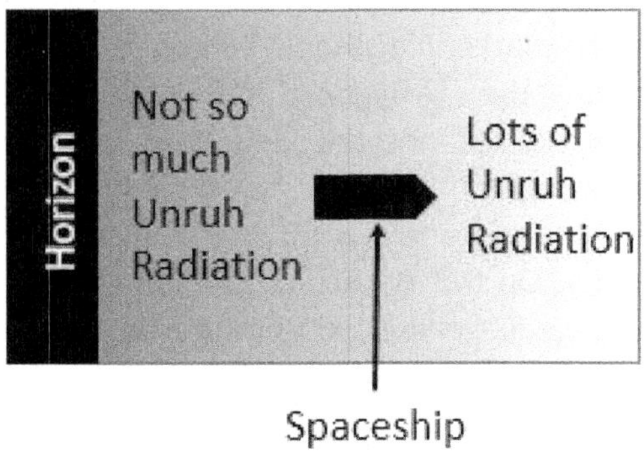

It is, very loosely, like a boat near a dock. There are more waves out to sea pushing it toward the dock than there are waves in the sheltered area between it and the dock pushing it back out, so it is slowly pushed towards the dock. The dock in this case is a horizon for the waves since it is a solid barrier to them and frictionally damps them when they are close. This effect has been known in nautical circles for centuries and is called the Maritime Casimir effect.

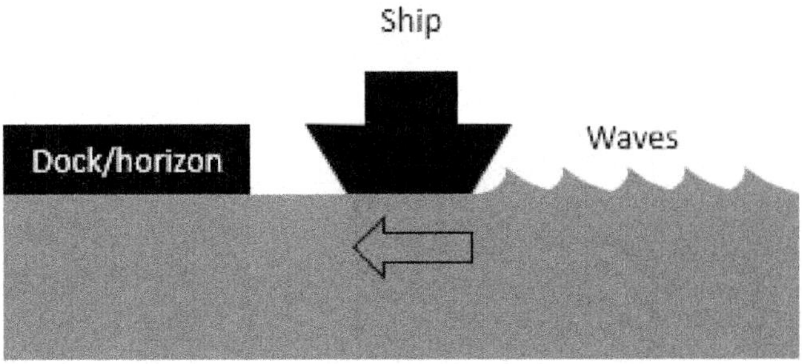

So why am I telling you all this? Well, it has its uses. This thermal Unruh radiation is all over the place, just like the waves on a sea, if we still had seas. It is even in the hardest vacuum of space. Very oddly in the way events conspire, the word unruh in German means noise – very apt for a vacuum vibration. What would happen to a boat if you suddenly damped the waves on only one side of it? Say, using a 'skirt'. There would be more waves pushing it from the other side and so it would move towards the damped side. Movement without fuel! What would happen to any object if you suddenly damped this radiation by putting a horizon above it? It would move upwards, without the need for rockets or propellant.

So, in my experiment I had a highly accelerated 'core' generating massive accelerations and therefore plenty of lovely acceleration-dependent Unruh waves, and then I had designed a metal structure that damps a broad spectrum of these waves above the object. The result was an Unruh gradient, lots of waves below, fewer above. The object should then fall upwards.

I switched it on, and for the fourth time in an hour, my Thrustbox zoomed upwards and banged into the ceiling, narrowly missing the foam I had stuck there to damp the impact. Not a loud bang, but my long-suffering neighbour reacted by banging on the floor. I was probably spoiling his immersion in a new seventh-dimensional virtual reality. Virtual tech was not banned, bread and circuses to keep the people inert, and was even encouraged. I shouted apologies, unable to hide the glee in my voice.

Chapter 3. Maati. Seaweed and other tragedies.

When my sister and I arrived at the seaweed farm, a network of metal grids with green plants bathed in purple light, we pushed off the floor in the low gravity, and rose quickly holding hands, up into the network of scaffolding that held the seaweed fast, giggling at each other conspiratorially.

The farm robots were hovering next to the weeds spraying mist on them like diminutive magicians. They spared us the occasional glance in irritation, chirping curiously to each other in the fast beep-and-click language they had developed of their own accord.

I worshipped my younger sister - I would never have told her of course. She was gorgeous, with her unusual long curly reddish hair, (most Inuit have jet black hair) and her large breasts. She had already driven several of the adolescent testosterone-doped boys in her class as crazy as headless chickens. One poor sod had recently stolen a space-tug and tried to see into her bedroom from outside the space station, several others poor sods, with a cleverer plan, had suddenly become very good at maths, and had been invited over for frustrating evenings they would never forget.

In contrast men gave me a wide berth, although I was similar in looks to my sister. I suppose they were deterred by my more serious character, but I loved her, everyone did, because she was incapable of an evil thought - some jealous friends of hers had said she was incapable of *any* thought, but I didn't agree: she had cleverly focused on utilising her looks to get a good man and have children. In our society, unlike in the decadent doomed regime that had existed before the Big Shift, which had denied the existence of women and their role, motherhood was valued highly.

Anyway, whereas I spent my evenings trying to memorise the Latin names of plant species she was being wined and dined by a vast array of panting men. Some of them quite handsome.

It was obvious where in the dome the seaweed was ready, because most of the hovering robots were congregated there, picking them up with their thin and dextrous arms and depositing them in baskets on their flat heads so we followed the commotion. As we approached this hive of robotic activity, they backed away in disorder, chirping even more to each other. Two hyperactive robots were attempting to pull away the same piece of weed, and some others had to intervene to stop a fight, cooing at the seething pair.

Linguists from the ever-curious European colony were still trying to translate this new robotic language, but it seemed to be evolving far faster than human languages. As soon as they had understood a subset, the language evolved again, leaving them helpless. Maybe it was deliberate? Would that be a new thing, a language designed by its speakers to be indecipherable?

Looking guiltily at each other we began peeling off a few strands of weed. The robots looked on, helpless to interfere with humans - this was part of their core programming. The weed was crisp and as salty as we had hoped. After a while, I asked a question I'd been meaning to ask for a while.

"So how is your mate to be? What's his name.. Ik Ulaq?"

Aniqa rolled her head from side to side as if to say so-so.

"Yes. Ik's OK. But I do wonder sometimes if he's for me. He's so friggin' unambitious. The other day at the junior Iditarod across Enceladus he almost came last - and didn't seem to mind. He just joined his mates in a weedbeer!"
"How terrible!" I said with false shock.
"Isn't it? I want a man with some raging fire in him, you know?"

She curled her hair around her ear as if to demonstrate how rapturous she was. She seemed to suffer some kind of internal indecision, then she spoke

"I haven't seen your poor sod for a while. What happened to him?"
"He buggered off...said I loved only robots, and I was as frigid as Enceladus."

Aniqa laughed, her mouth full of weed, shaking her head as if in despair.

"Ma and Pa, they keep asking me to persuade you to breed. They say you're letting the family down."

She grinned and recited from a recently popular poem that she liked but which scanned better in the original Inuit:

"Have children. In a thousand years you'll be a million among the stars!"

Our colonies were child-mad. We desperately needed to grow in population to survive the vindictive attacks from Terra and, being at the edge of the Solar System there was also the feeling that the cold universe needed to be colonised and warmed with human occupants. Although we had no technology capable of getting us across the mind-bending distance to the nearest star, Proxima Centauri we hoped we eventually would. Our society was on the edge, and efficiency was paramount, so the sexes had re-specialised to make the best use of their evolved talents. So men were expected to work hard and fight for their family and the colony and were trained from birth to do this, and women had a duty to procreate early, when it is healthy, and then train and nurture: so most were mothers first, then later in life teachers or medical doctors. We hated the ideas of identity & equality that had existed before the Big Shift in the individualistic culture that had damaged Terra in so many ways.

I garlanded my sister with seaweed mocking the traditional wedding ritual.

"I'm glad we have you to carry on the family line. I'll never get a mate."
"Oh. There's someone for everyone!"
"That may be true, but what if mine's on the frozen Terra?"
"Then destiny will move worlds to bring you together!"

That was when I noticed something moving beyond the dome against the slowly moving backdrop of stars. A small bright star was waxing there, coming from the direction of the cool white spot of the setting sun, reflecting its light. I assumed it to be one of the water-ferries from the nearby space station: the one that in the old days, when we were ruled by Terra, was called New Pittsburg, but was now named NeuHeim, "New home" in Pennsylvania Dutch.

There was a jag of intense white light, a disorientating noise and an abrupt gust of wind, and the seaweed suddenly became an organic chaos like a witch's hair in a hurricane. My ears popped and my eyes seemed to by trying to leave my skull. I opened my mouth and my lungs screamed in agony. The hydroponic dome above must have been breached by a projectile weapon. I tried to cling on to a flailing robot while grabbing my sister. The robot, straining to the maximum with his magnetics to drag us to safety, couldn't support us both, and when I lost hold we flew up towards the hole in the canopy and the cold vacuum, clinging on to each other. I tried to scream as a huge multi-coloured sphere appeared in front of us. It opened, like a fast growing giant tulip, and I found myself swallowed inside it, like a butterfly in a net. My ears popped as the pressure normalised, and I looked around frantically to find Aniqa. The sphere was transparent from the inside, and the sight of my sister, in panic, outside the sphere in the near vacuum, trying in vain to get inside with me broke my heart. Mercifully, I passed out.

I have no idea how long I was unconscious. I came to, wondering if it had all been a dream, but the noises I could hear were unfamiliar, and there was a smell of metal and disinfectant, and what was that pain in my ears and eyes? Probably caused by the near vacuum I'd experienced. I didn't want to open my eyes, so I tried to pretend that I was still comatose, but my captors, whoever they were, must have identified my conscious state, probably from my brain waves. Someone slapped my face, and I opened my eyes from the shock. There were two people, sun-burned Caucasians, Terrans, sat at the bed's end. A thin dark skinned middle-aged man in a suit, and a blonde woman in white. Aniqa was nowhere in sight.

"Where is my sister?" I screamed in our Inuit language. My voice was shredded and coarse. They looked at each other, and I quickly shook my head in irritation and repeated in English.
"Where is my sister?"
"We have a few questions," said the woman.
"About what? Who in hell are you?" I said.

I tried to lift my hands, which turned out to be rigidly strapped to the bed. Some crackpots on our station had claimed to have been abducted by Terrans and been sent back, but these claims had quickly evaporated after the claimers were bought a few weed-beers. The woman leaned forwards, her face full of concern.

“We’re from Terra. I should remind you that the space station you occupy is United Nations property, and you people are there illegally according to article 23.1 of the New World Constitution. Terra is now ready to reoccupy the station, but we mean no harm. We just need information. Population figures, hierarchies, leaders, naval strength.. That sort of thing.”

I felt tears burning at the back of my eyes.

“Tut tut.” she said a smile played around the corners of her mouth. To my surprise she switched effortlessly to Inuit.

“Look dear. Life could be very easy, or indescribably difficult, for you. Just provide us with information and we’ll take you home. Why should a young lady like you be harmed?”
“I don’t trust you. I’ve heard things.”
“You’ve been misinformed, we are only doing this for the good of the colonies. You would be far better with a proper administrator appointed from Terra.”
“Like before, when they used to Euthanase us?”
“Those were the old days. Things are different now.”

I studied the man next to her for a while. He had a very handsome face. Perfectly symmetrical, but his eyes looked like they had ice forming in them.

"Who is the man next to you? Does he talk?"

She nervously looked around at him, with a mix of fear and distaste.

"He's a political officer. Sent here just in case you aren't co-operative."

He gazed at me calmly, and spoke in a studiedly-friendly manner in English.

"I have an expertise in extracting information from aliens."
"Sounds painful. How do you do it? Through the nose?"

His smile widened, still asymmetric.

"We apply electromagnetic waves to the brain to induce a co-operative state. It's an old method, but I like its efficiency. Though such procedures can induce severe damage to the neurons, so my nice colleague here would like to avoid that. You can avoid that by being co-operative."
"So, if I don't co-operate, you'll fry my brain. Is that it?"

He smiled with obvious difficulty.

"You have a wit about you. Would be a shame to lose it."
"Isn't this immoral?"
"Morality only applies to humans. You're an alien."
"How convenient for you!"

"Isn't it?"

He looked amused, except his eyes. His colleague looked at him in concern and then at me in sympathy.

"Don't worry. I sure you'll be a good girl. We have laws that delay the use of mind probes for a few weeks. Even for aliens. Why not cooperate?"

Chapter 4. Dork. Astronomy and sex.

The first day I heard about Maati it was early January. Not that the old European seasons meant a rats' bundle in the new Africa, and New Cambridge was being drenched by a weak tropical storm that had formed in what was left of the Indian ocean. The town was built comprehensively. All the old Cambridge colleges, with their quaint ancient names, had been reproduced in their original styles: sandstone gothic, brick, post-modern, Islamic, organic, but in view of the humid, tropical climate with its torrential rain and floods, they had been built on stilts, with steeply sloping roofs and tall metal lightning conductors to keep the lights on. From dreaming spires to dreaming spikes.

When I arrived at work, at 10am, my gorgeous office colleague, Lark, a Scot by ethnicity, was already well into her day, and sat there looking bloody serious as usual, and reading the University newspaper: The Isis. She was seated calmly and indifferently at me, in the way that only women can do, with her legs crossed. Her dark hair cascaded down her bulging front. As ever, she was covered minimally because of the humidity, and, as on most morning of the past two years, I lost most of what little common sense I had. She looked up.

"Oh Dorkmouse! Nice o' you to turn up, afore we all go home."

She smiled her "I know-what-you're-bloody-thinking-and-forget-it" smile causing my ears to radiate heat, and glanced at the newspaper, then back up at me.

"Hey, you're interested in those colonists near Jupiter aren't you?"
"Saturn!"
"OK. Have a look at the news!"

Deftly, she wafted the holographic paper towards me, and then stood up, stretched sensuously, and grabbed her illegal and priceless antique British Bulldog mug.

"Why don't we go to the pagoda right now? Remember last Monday?"
"Will you stop it? Read the paper...or, here's a revolutionary suggestion: do some ruddy work!"
"Oh come on, life's short and brutish!" I said.
"It is in this office. Look, there is more to life than me and the pagoda."
"Like what?"

She gave me a motherly look.

"Dorkmouse, you seem to think about space and sex and that's it!"
"You seem to imply that's a bad thing?"
"Lazy Dorkmouse. Astronomy and sex: two things you can do lying down?"
"No, it's because they are both brilliant and fun...I can prove it."

"You know sex is frowned on. The New World constitution says *Emotional ties are discouraged because they undermine the authority of the state*."
"Don't remind me."
"Anyway. Many thanks for the offer, I'm sure it was heartfelt. Look, have a glance a' the news! Page D. It's space-related and might mention your hero Korentsev!" she said with mock awe.
"Kudravtsev!"

Still annoyed of course, but mildly interested, I looked at the holographic image of the news program which was now floating helpfully in front of my red face. It stated that the newly reconstituted World Space Force had been exploring near Saturn's icy moon Enceladus when they had been the victims of an unprovoked attack by a rebel space craft. They had of course retaliated and damaged a base of the rebels, and brought a few deformed specimens back for questioning. One of them, a female, was shown briefly in such an aggressive pose that it was difficult to see whether she was deformed or not. There was no mention of Kudravtsev.

I waved my hand down through the holonews and it disappeared.

"Hey! Some colonists are back on Terra! I'd like to have a chat with them."
"Yes, and if female you could fit both hobbies into one interview."

I giggled at this.

"What a good idea!"
"Well, talk to some of your drossy bosses – they might want a tech as an interviewer, the authoritarian bastards."

Lark was often on her high horse about something political or world-encircling. She was a Green: a group who believed that humanity was a danger to the planet. They perhaps had a point but the Big Crustal Shift had happened so suddenly and so brutally that it had made us feel a little inconsequential. It was quite a shock to the old-style greens. The new greens had shifted tack, but I disliked their anti-science attitude. Science creates problems, but then it solves then and if we stop that process we remain stuck in the latest problem.

Lark's work involved suppressing animal drug testing - a more noble form of suppression, she claimed, and I agreed. Although she was a Green, she was not as rabidly anti-science and she did occasionally say some insightful things. Often saying, as now:

"Dorkmouse, you're a mystery to me, with your dreams of interstellar travel. Why don't you ever do anything about it? You're pissing on your own bonfire."

She walked off to get some coffee, wiggling her hips as she went. She glanced over her shoulder at me with a darkly smouldering look, and raised the mug.

"Do you want some?"
"Yes!"
"I was referring to the coffee!"

She laughed and shook her head despairingly. I'd often wondered how Lark got away with expressing her ideas so forcefully. They went way beyond the official line. Maybe the authorities reasoned that a dog allowed to bark was unlikely to bite. Anyways, after cooling myself off, by pacing the room, and imagining cold, blue glaciers crashing into what was left of the Atlantic from the Moroccan coast, I sat down and caught myself thinking of philosophy rather than technical issues. This is something I had caught myself doing quite often during the past week. Philosophy: I avoided it these days as being painful - too much and I began to hate myself, and my job, and who wants that? One must earn a living.

I began leafing through some information on covert antigravity research that was still being done, mostly by the Russian refugee population in their town of Lotka, in southern India, and the Germans in Königsberg, in the Cameroon, and of course, probably in the Saturn colonies, and a quote from Gandhi that Lark often berates me with flashed through my head:

Happiness is when what you think, say and do, all agree.

My job was to seek out and find anti-gravity research, and inform those who could put a stop to it. It was tragic, and I was angry with myself, because I deeply wanted to help mankind get into deep space. As a child I'd had an epiphany reading a book of Greg Bear's called The Forge of God – it sounds terribly religious, but it isn't at all – and I believe, that Terra has sacrificed its ecosystem to give its intelligent offspring, us, a chance to take Terran life into space. Like a flower sacrificing and devoting all its energy to produce seeds. But, of course, we hadn't made it very far into space, after all the millions of years of evolution to produce us. We seeds had stayed at home. The Saturn colonies looked in danger of being destroyed by the new space activities of the world government, which seemed to have no colonising ideas of its own.

I averted the painful thought that I had no free will over the big issues at all, stopped myself thinking altogether, and to prove I had retained free will over something, I went to find Lark.

Chapter 5. Maati. Terror on Terra.

They brought me to Terra which looked different to the holograms I had poured over in class. From space, instead of a beautiful patchwork of blue and green, the planet was a cracked white and grey, rather like Enceladus. As Morley and I had often seen through our telescope, only the double rings of green, one north, and one south of the equator, remained as refuges for life, and there were a few sea-lets where oceans had once been, around the equator. The equator itself was shrouded by a belt of white convective thunder clouds in which there were intermittent flashes of lightning.

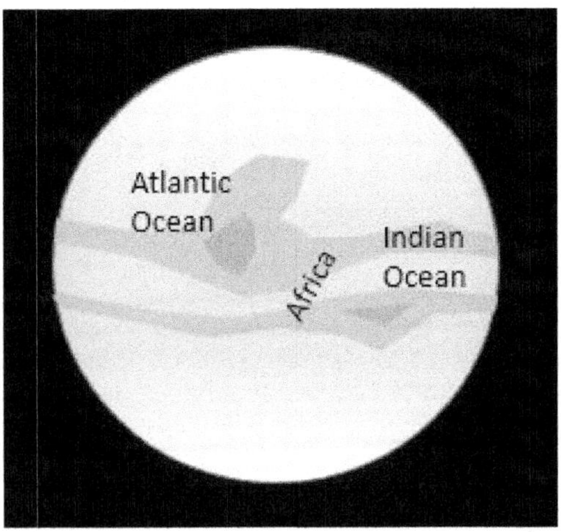

As I stepped out of the spacecraft onto the hot tarmac a recoiled from the massive boiler in the sky. The sun was far too bright, and frighteningly large: near Saturn the Sun is only a bright star. I immediately ran into the shade under the spacecraft wing and some hefty marines had to drag me out, laughing.

Being out in the open after a lifetime in a space station was not such a shock since I had walked in a space suit in open space back at the colony many times, but the air was sauna like. I sweated like a pig, and could hardly think. The gravity was stronger too and the air smelt of what turned out to be soil and petroleum. Do you get the impression I didn't like the place? Well, it wasn't all bad. After I'd signed myriad forms, with a made up name, and been thrown in a cell I took to watching the clouds through my cell window. This was satisfying, and the dense forest on the horizon formed waves in the strong winds.

One morning I was woken early by the torrential sunshine streaming through my cell window, the shadows of the bars making a curved pattern over my legs. I felt the door latch click and my guard came in with breakfast. He was black and I had never seen such a person before, except in old films. Very few made it to the colonies since Africa hadn't had a space program, so I was fascinated by his natural grace and jollity. The soily smell of Terra coffee, and of eggs and bacon reached me. I sat up on the bed, peering at the meal.

"I've been told to tell you to hurry it up! You've another meeting today."

I picked up the tray and began to eat. He sat down by the door, with his stun whip in his hand, took out a portable holo-player and spent five minutes trying to get it to work, as I ate my breakfast. Eventually he gave up and stared idly at me. I decided to try and mine him for information.

"Alright." I said, "What depraved monster am I meeting today?"

He seemed pleased I'd interrupted his boredom, but was disappointingly succinct.

"A scientist."
"That bad huh?"
"He's a space bozo. He's harmless enough. Wouldn't say boo to a goose."

I sipped my drink. Coffee on Terra was far richer in taste, maybe because of the stronger natural sunlight they had. Half an hour later I was shuffled into a room, clanking like a ghost in an old movie in my chains. The room was an unimaginative box, without windows and the scientist sat in it behind a table. I took to him straight away since he was so obviously out of his depth. In fact as soon as he saw me he leaned back and then dropped most of his papers on the floor and spent a few minutes picking them up again. He was reasonably good looking, with dark wavy hair and a narrow aquiline face, but from the lazy way he sat he did not appear to be disciplined or tough, both of which are qualities expected of men in our society. I was strapped opposite him into what I suppose could have been charitably called a chair, but resembled a cross between a straight-jacket and something Leonardo da Vinci could have dreamed up if he'd ever been employed by the Spanish inquisition. They fixed me into the chair, which was ill-fitting since it was designed to house massive criminals.

"Thank you so much!" I said to them ironically as they left. I'm sure the humour was lost on them.
"Er, hello." said the scientist holding a pen in front of him with two hands to attract my attention, or perhaps to ward me off.
"I'm Dr Dork Stratoe from the K Institute in New Cambridge."
"What does the K stand for?"
"It was originally named after Kudravtsev – after he escaped to space they changed it just to the initial."
"Oh, yes. I know Kudravtsev well."

There was a dull thudding sound as the listening technician in the next room fell off his chair in surprise and delight at the first bit of useful information they had extracted from me in two weeks. Dr Yevgeni Kudravtsev was a Russian space engineer. During the Big Shift and the Climate Wars, he had secretly built spacecraft for some Europeans, Russians and Chinese, and had led them in a daring Trek from Terra. They had escaped, fighting against Terra ships all the way, to the safety of our Inuit-Amish mining colonies.

I had an intuition about this scientist, who seemed genuinely interested in space and, surprisingly, me also. He, Dork, cleared his throat

"He's still alive then? He must be close to ninety now."

So, he wasn't completely besotted with me. He was still capable of being sceptical. My respect for him rose a little.

"People live longer in the colonies." I said, "We use only 0.7g."
"That's odd. Your bones show no osteoporosis."
"We exercise a lot, and we eat a lot of fish for calcium and Vitamin D. You should try it some time."
"That would be difficult. Not many fish left here."

He looked rather glum at this, then asked.

"Has Dr Kudravtsev made any advances?"
"No, of course not. He's a decent man!"

He froze, puzzled, and then he managed a smile.

"No, er, I meant technical advances, not personal ones."
"Oh. I understand. Sorry, my poor English."
"I'm just interested that's all. I've read all about him."
"It's odd to find someone interested in innovation in a place like this."

He glanced at me from lowered eyes, and almost looked as if he was about to weep. I was embarrassed for him, but oddly affected. He then made a valiant effort to rally, probably realising he'd made a mistake and I was now interrogating him.

So I really started to interrogate him, while I could.

"Are you an engineer?"
"I'm a physicist, or was..."
"So what are you now?"

The level of his gaze dropped. I liked him. He was shy, and seemed sensible, but he was about as comfortable with interrogation as I would have been at seduction, or Einstein would have been behind a machine gun. He held his hand to his ear, listening to an implant there. His overseers had also realised that I was now interrogating him. He looked at me, said

"Bollocks...er. Sorry. My time is up. I hope we can meet again, in a more," he looked at my chair, "relaxed state. I genuinely have many questions."
"Why can't they tell me where my sister is?" I frowned.

At this he looked extremely uneasy.

"I'm very sorry, I'm just a tech. I'll try to ask someone for you."

As I was led away by my pet thugs I decided I had to at least try to escape.

Chapter 6. Dork. Dreams.

I woke up, at 2am, to the usual incessant sound of tropical rain fretting on my window, mixed with distant thunder, and investigated my tattered mosquito net, unable to sleep in the humidity. I had just dreamed about the girl I'd interviewed a few days before. She had been a sight for sore eyes, pale and serious as she had been. I imagined her hair and her rugged looks. Her face was broad and almost Mongolian, despite her reddish hair colour, and being rather thin and physically weak myself, I'd always been attracted to broad and physically strong females. I sighed.

In my dream the girl was being tortured by insectoid machines on a table. Somehow I'd managed to set up my inertial modification experiment around the table and had blasted her through the ceiling. With the illogic of dreams she had somehow grabbed hold of me on her way up, and we had both shot up into space, and started to make love on a bed of roses and fish in zero gravity. This, of course, is when the mosquito net's support bar fell on my head and woke me up. I mumbled to myself as I rearranged the net

"Dork... you'd bite off more than you could chew with that one."

Chapter 7. Ngala Mbo. Jazz Café.

On orders, I frequented his bar for a few nights to allay suspicion, before I went to speak to him. He looked like a man attempting to drink himself into oblivion. As the pianoman started a rendition of a Hornsby classic, I approached his table, enjoying the syncopated rhythms, and sat down next to him.

"Good day, Sir. May I sit here," I said.

He looked up at me through his dark fringe and raised eyebrows.

"Sure." he said.

I looked at the bottles lined up neatly like terms in an equation.

"Wow. There must a girl behind all this alcohol. Or something else?"

"I'm destroying the thing that I love."
"What is that then?"
"Inertial theory."
"A funny thing to love."

He paused to smile at that.

"Yes, you're quite right."

"Well, man, maybe you ought to stop loving abstract ideas and start loving people eh? It's what God made us for."
"I'm doing that too. There's a girl.."
"Of course."
"See that red haired girl on the news? From the outworld? I interrogated her a few days ago."

I feigned concern

"Are you with the CIA or something?"
"No. I was asked to interview her as a technical expert. I messed it up."
"So. No torture?"
"No."
"Good man. So what was she like?"
"Very attractive. I thought she'd be deformed or something."
"She may be dead now, you know?"

He looked as if he was about to burst into tears at this and I made the decision.

"Do you know that I lied just then? She is actually been held in a hospital not far from here: in a town called Gondar, close to the Tana glacier. She attempted to escape and the guards shot her up quite badly, but she survived and is in stem cell therapy. Now, Dr Dork Stratoe."

He looked up at this.

“How do you know my full name?”

“We know your name well through your papers. Would you like to meet some friends of mine?”

Chapter 8. Dork. The hole in the wall.

Finding out that the girl was still alive decided me. I suddenly decided that I'd lived long enough, my future was shortening, and I may as well go out following the right course. So via Ngala, I made contact with the resistance ('them') and after that there was no turning back. It was to be a hospital break.

I went to see my manager at the K Institute: Dr Peck. My relationship with him was complex. When I had been forcibly re-educated many years ago, he had agreed to take me on, as a once-promising, but now discredited and burned out rank and file scientist. I was grateful for that. But, he was the sort of man who does well in every regime. He was clever, but not creative, and had a rigidity that was impossible to crack. He could recite whole sections of the New World Constitution at us, and often did when we often tried to reason with him. He also had the ability to drain the life out of me like an enthusiasm-vampire. I knocked on the open door, and stepped into his large office:

"Hello Dork, did you check in with my secretary?"
"No."
"Well, you should have done. Anyway, you're here now...I hope you've recovered from your encounter with the alien?"
"Yes." I lied.
"Good. I've read that review you wrote on the history of inertia. Very interesting for specialists, but your enthusiasm shows in some of your prose and I think you ought to be careful you

don't become one of the people we're looking for. Ha ha!"

I felt the familiar feeling of encroaching frustration, of cancelling myself out.

"Dork. You know, as well as I do that the powers that be don't need new blue skies work, so what is the point of you wasting your time on it? Remember the contract you signed? That is an important commitment."

I screamed at myself internally, and knew he felt he was being reasonable, but that is not the same as being right. I had the same feeling of being a singer confined to a Trappist monastery. However, today, this futile conversation, oft repeated, seemed different. It was as if I'd been smashing my head on a door for years to no avail, then suddenly realised there was a window in the adjacent wall. People had left Terra, and survived, 40 years ago. Free people did exist. I'd decided to do anything, even lie, to get out to them.

"You're right." I lied.

Peck sat back and basked in the sunlight emanating from his status, and was apparently unaware that I was lying. He then gazed lovingly at an animated hologram of his wife blowing him a kiss, on his desk. After a short pause I said

"I want to see the colonist again. I have a question that might trip her."

There was a dangerous pause at that, but he recovered quickly

"Do you? Interesting! Have our people verified it?"
"No."
"Well, I think they'd better. Then if it's acceptable I'll get you sorted."

Chapter 9. Dr Peck. Resistance is futile.

That day I watched Dork walk out of the room with mixed feelings. It was obvious to me what he wanted. He wanted the girl, but also, he wanted what she could give him: the chance to get off planet and make a genuine contribution to research and advance mankind. It was very noble, but the time for nobility was long past. One had to survive. For years he'd understood this, been a coward, like the rest of us, doing what he was told. Now he'd decided to break free, and it was obvious to me he would be dead in a short time. They always were. I'd seen it happen too many times. To some much cleverer than Dork. He was too naive to realise that it was plainly obvious to me, and the military police, what was going on in his head. I called my American operative, now, of course, based in New Pittsburg in Costa Rica."

"Hello Brad. Peck, K Institute here."
"Peck! How goes id?"
"Looks like one of mine is about to fly."
"He has a homing device fitted, yeah?"
"Yes."
"No problem then. He'll lead us to some interesting folk."

Chapter 10. Maati. Hospital discharge.

Some of the Terrans' medical technology was more advanced than ours. I didn't realise we had fallen behind. Perhaps it was the fact that our space station's environment is sterile compared with the teeming multitudes of Terra bacteria. Anyway, after I'd tried to escape by hitting my guard with the detached U-tube from my sink and had been shot, they'd injected some of my own stem cells, extracted apparently from my bone marrow. Over a couple of weeks these had then grown to replace the damaged parts of my stomach, and within a week the hole in my stomach, and all the pain had gone. Like dear Morley back home, part of me had been replaced.

One morning I opened my eyes, noticing that the usual smell of disinfectant had been tempered by something else, and there was my former interviewer, sat at the foot of my bed, studiously reading a holobook suspended in the air while he waited for me to wake up. I watched him for nearly ten minutes before he became aware that I was awake, and then he looked up, startled.

"Sorry." he said, and tried to smile. He moved his chair, squeaking it along the floor, closer to my head, the holobook followed him, and he glanced nervously at the huge guard stood in solemn boredom by the door. He stared at me for a good few minutes, as if trying to apologise without making a sound. Eventually, he spoiled the moment by opening his mouth.

“How are the stem cells going?”

I pulled up my night shirt to show him my stomach.

“Good medicine. You lead us in some things.”

He looked at my stomach, swallowed as if holding back an impulse. When nothing emerged I asked,

“What is going to happen to me?”
“Re-education. They put an implant in your head that causes discomfort whenever you have an illegal thought. Eventually you learn to avoid such thoughts habitually, and become a model citizen. Pavlovian.”

He suddenly leaned over and kissed me on the ear, then leaned back and said.

“Sorry. I couldn’t help it.”

The guard coughed mildly, and was looking at us obliquely in amusement. Then, remarkably, Dork began speaking without moving his lips.

“Please look normal. I’ve planted a small speaker in your ear. This is a rescue. Noble, eh? I’ve made some rather dangerous contacts among the local, er, Upstarts they call themselves. The authorities, I suspect, know all this, and will let us go safely because they wish us to lead them to some more important people. Hopefully, they don't know that we know that they know."

I smiled, as if responding to the kiss. The voice in my head continued.

"Smile if you are OK to go. If you don't, then I'll come back in a few days."

I smiled rather too broadly and hurt my cheeks.

"If you smiled, I am now going to fire a small dart at the guard by the door."

I tried not to look surprised as he pulled out a pen, and aimed it at the guard who had been smiling to himself, and who now suddenly clutched his arm, eyes wide in surprise and fell in a crumpled heap by the door. His chair also bounced loudly in the other direction. We looked at each other expecting a response to the noise, but no one came. Dork dashed over and grabbed the guard's stun whip, then took off his outer clothes to reveal those of a doctor.

"I'm a doctor of Physics", he said, "which requires 6 years of training: BSc and PhD. Now I've temporarily demoted myself to a doctor of medicine: they only study for five years, you see." He looked at my surprised face and said
"Just boasting...physicist's pride. Oh, the guard is just asleep.

Don't worry."
"I wasn't worried. I'm surprised at your boldness, that's all."
"What do you mean?"
"You didn't seem very decisive when we last met."

He looked appealingly dejected for a moment, then tried to lighten the mood.

"I've been having decisiveness lessons from the Upstarts, and I must admit they were so shocked by my schlemiel tendencies that they encouraged me to take amphetamines. I did. Come on! Put on this overcoat, and let's go. We have to stay ahead of events!"

He grabbed my arm and helped me out of bed. Suddenly fairies and stars paraded through wild mazes in my head as the blood drained out of it. So we paused for a few moments while my pulmonary system pumped some back in. We then walked nonchalantly out of the room into the corridor outside. He grabbed my arm and we turned right and arrived at an elevator. A bored nurse was waiting by the door. Luckily she hadn't seen me before, but she examined us suspiciously. The doors opened and we all walked in.

"Which floor?" said the nurse.
"Lower ground." Said Dork.

I grabbed his hand, and looked demurely at the nurse, who, looked away and smiled. I'd convinced her that our trip to the lower ground was nothing more than a romantic escape.

The nurse got out at the ground floor, winked at me and sighed.

"Young love!"

With a sentimental grin she was gone. Dork seemed not to appreciate or notice the little bit of psychology I had just used – typical man. A few seconds later the door opened on the lower ground floor. Piles of clothes hulked in the darkness, and the air was even more humid than usual: it was the hospital laundry. Banks of washing machines were lined up along the walls, some in noisy operation.

Dork began dragging me down the corridor, but I pulled him up short, uncertain about where we were going.

"Wait a minute!" I said, "I hope you have a good plan?"
"Yes, but it depends on us getting ourselves down this corridor quickly."
"Why?"
"Because..."

Suddenly, the air in the laundry was split radially out by a chemical explosion, and when the air smashed together again there was a bang that flung us to the floor. A cloud of smoke rushed past us and it should have been followed by the pitter-patter of bits of debris falling back to Terra, but I'd gone deaf. Dork pulled himself up and dusted himself down. My ears popped.

"...because of that! Now we have to go the other way!"

This time I didn't argue, and followed him as we ran through the hole in the wall of the laundry, already very wet because of the incessant tropical rain. Down the flooded and humid empty street came an electric car, almost silent. It splashed to a halt opposite us, and the back door opened. A woman's voice shouted,

"Get in!"

I looked at the front seat.

"No-one is driving!"
"Of course not." She said "You been frozen for the last few decades?"

Dork pushed me in, pilled in on top, and I was pressed back into the seat by the acceleration. Soon we were past the ranks of apartment blocks. The quality of the road surface declined and we were in a far more primitive, but more aesthetic settlement. Wooden shacks were lit from within in a friendly way. The woman was looking out of the back window, holding a gun. A little while later, after we had been bounced around like dice in a box, the pace slowed, and the woman turned to face us and offered her hand.

“It seems we have no tailers. I’m Ndala. How would you like a trip to space?”

Chapter 11. Dork. Sex on the beach.

That night we went into hiding in the African port of Gondar, and we were confident that the authorities would not pounce on us, until we had made contact with more important dissidents in former Tanzania. The Africans held a dance on the beach in our honour. The Moon shone over the sea and Orion was up – on its side as usual at the Equator. It was interesting to see the effect on Maati, since apparently neither dance, nor music were common in the Saturn colonies. Apparently the colonists had some CDs, mostly of pre-20th century classical music, so the African rhythms were very different.

Everyone was in a jovial mood. I felt a hero after having rescued Maati. She also looked pretty good to me, as Ndala tried to teach her a rhumba. I have two interests: sex and space, and she represented, as Lark had predicted, both of them combined.

Sergio was ecstatic to see Maati free. He was a large, self-confident, Mexican, and was part of a rapidly growing group keen to stimulate space exploration. They were called the Upstarts, so he was eager to speak to Maati. After we had eaten some African bread and consumed German Weissbeer, we sat down, each with a glass to discuss the day's events. Sergio was ready with questions.

"So Maati. We know nothing about your home!"

Maati, put down her glass.

"Can I really trust you? Maybe this is just a set up to get me to talk?"
"You're right. It is a set-up. We want you to talk, but we're the good guys!"
"Well, I find it hard to believe that the CIA would be using someone as naïve as Dork here", she said with an affectionate smile in my direction.
"I'm not sure how to take that!"
"OK. My home. We are surviving. We are maybe 10,000 Inuit, 10,000 Amish a few thousands Russians, Europeans and a few Chinese. We live on space stations orbiting Enceladus. We are having a few problems. For example, our weed farms, sorry, that's seaweed, keep failing, we have a theory that this is because the bacterial ecosystem we have is not varied enough, so while I'm here I intend to collect a sample of your lake water – the murkier the better."
"OK. I'll arrange a sterile sample bottle..."
"I wouldn't bother with sterile, just bung a lot of dirty lake water in. Our labs will have a field day if we ever get back..."
"How about your culture? Is it old capitalist, communist?"
"I'd say far more traditional and collective than here. The old capitalist regimes were far too individualistic in our view, and it seems here some of that has been retained. We think far more of the good of the group, but also we seem to be freer. No one would dream of silencing Dork here for example."

Sergio nodded, saying

"You can say whatever you want?"
"Yes. Essential for a proper debate on any subject, for the good of the group. This of course leads to arguments, and fights, but the losers are tolerated. We have space for new ideas and groups to grow."
"You are forming new colonies?"
"The Amish are. Their fertility rate is amazing. They have to build an entirely new space station every few months. Some of them live near Jupiter now."
"Do you have faster than light travel?"
"No, but I was just talking to Dork here and he has some ideas on that. It would be great if he would come with me and I could introduce him to Kudravtsev. Travelling to the Proxima Centauri system or further has always been one of our goals, and it would be the best way to escape attacks from Terra."

Sergio turned to me.

"Dork. You've come this far. Are you willing to go all the way?"
"It scares me to death, but it's always been my dream, so... Also, there's nothing for me here."

I didn't get involved in the conversation much after that, since as I looked at Maati's rounded figure I was working on another sort of proxima.

Ecstatically for me, as the Moon sank over the lake, everyone else mooched off to the shacks at the back of the beach, and

Maati and I were nearly alone with the light surf. I had been abstaining from drink for most of the night, so I was sober. She was almost asleep, but still holding a glass of red wine in her hands, resting it on her stomach. In the soft light from a lone beach lamp beside her, I could see the shadows formed by her breasts.

I am aware that the male love of large breasts and wide hips is an evolutionary development, in that we are programmed to choose women who are likely to be able to give birth easily (wide hips) and feed children most effectively (large breasts) in order to give our genes a good chance of survival. Nevertheless, such women are still beautiful things to behold and besides, knowing the why does not dull the enjoyment of doing.

Maati was wearing a white T-shirt and shorts and her long dark red hair cascaded down her front like a dark waterfall. I moved, so that I was looking down at her, and decided to try out the Inuit I had learned:

"Nagligigavet!" I was assuming that she would be flattered by my use of her language. Her eyes, brown, opened and looked at me.
"Nice try."

Her eyes closed again. Luckily I had, earlier that evening trawled through the internet in search of romantic Inuit poems, and had found one by a poet called Uvavnuk. I held the piece of paper I'd written the poem on up and recited it.

"The great sea moves me, sets me adrift.
The vault of heaven moves me.
Mighty weather storms through my soul.
It carries me with it.
Trembling with joy."

A snoring sound emerged from Maati. I was just beginning to regret my choice of poem, and contemplate waking her up when she giggled and opened her eyes again.

"One of our sayings.." she said ".. is don't flatter the foot, just kiss it."
"I'd settle for that!"
"For that you can kiss me."

I did, and all my frustration disappeared in relief. My hand wandered instinctively to her breast. She then stood up, and with the wild look in her eyes, that only women seem to manage, she took of her T-shirt revealing breasts that curved outwards to the nipple, and wobbled as she laughed at my expression. She then sat down on my lap thrusting her warm, dry breasts into my face as the surf played with itself at the beach edge.

The rest was too beautiful to confine to the page. Suffice it to say, that I fell in love with her so strongly that the rest of this story became possible.

Chapter 12. Maati. All the way.

We were lying in the warm gentle ebb and flow of the surf after the event. We were both in that tender state when nothing else seems to matter. I was lying on him, clinging to him to try and feel safe, but I didn't. We had a long way to go to get home.

"Dork?"
"Yes." He said, almost asleep,
"Am I just sex for you, or will you go all the way?"

I waited for him to stiffen. My sister always said that this always happens when men have to commit. He didn't stiffen though, and thought about his reply, which was so dated as to be almost prehistoric.

"You are a beautiful flower I've just found growing from a pavement. I intend to go with you with a club and knock out anyone who might stand on you."

I thought about this.

"What if they are bigger than you? It is quite likely isn't it?"
"Hey! I'm not that small," he said, with indignation.
"What if you had to leave Terra with me, for ever!" I said.

There was a long pause after this.

"I love you and your fantastic body, and also I want to see people who are optimistic like you and who are able to escape from convention across boundaries whenever they want. So, yes. I'll go."

Chapter 13. Dork. Debug.

The sun rose with a fantastic demonstration of light refraction, or as Maati called it, in wonder: a burning sky. We awoke with an impatient Sergio sitting next to us and flicking sand playfully on us.

"Buenos Dias! Time to escape from this pebble to the sky!"

Maati's tousled hair appeared from beneath a blanket.

"How?"
"With the help of Dr Stratoe there."
"I suppose you expect me to take off vertically like Superman?"
"Yes. I'll say no more now except we have commissioned a fishing boat to take you out onto the Tana Hayk lake."
"A fishing boat? We have the world's police after us, we need to get into space, and we're going fishing? How Louis Armstrong."
"Ocean travel and space travel are similar, differing by only one extra dimension."

This comment was true, but quite unhelpful. Sergio then became very serious.

"However, before we go we have to disable the implant they put into Maati."

Maati rubbed her eyes,

"Oh yes? How are you going to do that?"
"We'll sedate you, and then electrocute you. That should short it out. In the meantime we'll set up a dummy implant that emits the same signal. This will buy us a few hours of time in which to move."

Maati grimaced slightly.

"Won't the electricity short me out too?"
"No, we'll take care not to disrupt your heart."

I was not happy about this. In my experience, whenever something has gone well, it has always been followed by a disaster of equal magnitude, and the previous night had gone fantastically well.

"I'm not too keen on this. Is it necessary?"

Sergio was indignant

"Yes! The only reason they have allowed us to continue this far, despite knowing where we are, is because they hope we will lead them to more of us. If we take her anywhere while broadcasting they will just follow, even into space. We have to move undetected, or not at all!"

Maati stood up holding the blanket around her.

"Sergio's right."
"But what if you die?"
"Then you should continue to try to get of the planet. If you succeed my life won't have been in vain. You really should have a word about your interstellar theories with Kudravtsev, and take some muck with you."
"I'll hold Sergio responsible if you're harmed."

Sergio seemed slightly amused.

"Either you are still drugged and dangerous, or you have fallen in love and are even more dangerous! She'll be fine. Now, can we get on with it?"

It was worse than watching someone you loved having their heart restarted, because this dangerous procedure was being performed, not to save the victim's life, but to ensure the safely of all of us. After it had finished, and an hour later when Maati came out of her sleep, I was in such a state of mind that I would have done anything for her. All she wanted, she said, was for me to help her get home, and come home with her. I looked up. Easier said than done.

Chapter 14. Dork. The Bad Ass.

Our ship, called, in a very African manner, the Bad Ass, was a large fishing vessel that worked its way up and down the Tana Hayk lake. It was moored at a grimy dock in Gondar, a shanty town which extended right to the pristine white beach we had partied on, crowded with fishing boats, both traditional African types and modern. Rising high above the African town were the apartment blocks of the European settlement, reaching 40 stories towards the sky.

We were hurried on board by Fisherman Mbeki. I was amused to see the difficulty they had in casting the boat off from the dock. This was the Maritime Casimir effect. There was some wind and the waves on the lake were choppy. There were of course more waves out to sea, than in the sheltered area between the ship and the dock. This caused a net wave-push on the boat towards the dock. This was a brilliant metaphor for how the horizon drive works and I explained it to Maati.

Mbeki showed us our cabins, and virtually pushed us into them, then hurried off. Presumably he had spoken to the captain, or he *was* the captain, and a few minutes later the Bad Ass moved slowly out onto the lake into the rain.

A few minutes later Maati appeared in the doorway of my cabin, and held her leg up against the wall by the door like an Inuit Marlene Dietrich.

"Are you pleased to see me?"
"Yes, I could eat you!" I said, truthfully.

Then there appeared, in the doorway behind her, a massive fellow with grey hair and the manner and clothing of a vagabond. The incongruity of him standing next to Maati made me laugh, and he frowned, and stuffed his hands in his pockets. When he spoke he did so in a clipped manner.

"I captain of the Bass Ass." he said.

Maati jumped half a mile at this, as she hadn't noticed him. I stuck out my hand for him to shake, as Maati turned, saw him, and glanced at me nervously, as if expecting me to protect her from attack.

"We don't have time for introductions. We have an antigravity device on this ship. It's crude, but you should be able to work out how it operates, since I'm told you developed some of the theory for it years back – yes, yes, we read your papers! All you have to do is get into the damn thing and launch it. It'll go up, and you'll be met in space by a small fleet of Outlanders - we've been in touch - provided they haven't been attacked by a Terra fleet before then."

"What if they have?"
"Then you will be lost in space. I'd advise you both to have a last fling."
"You don't beat about the bush do you!"

As if to prove this, he ignored the comment

"We intend to launch damn soon. We've warned your fleet of this," he said blandly. Maati's eyes looked as if they were about to pop out.

"That's wonderful!"
"No. Bad Ass!" said the captain with a sudden smile "Your fleet are not that far off, and at the speed of light, our message should get to them in three minutes. I don't know how long it will take for them to get back here. They wouldn't tell us much. They could be riding in wooden barrels for all I know."
"Taking acceleration into account, about five hours or more." said Maati "we can travel close to 1% the speed of light, maximum."

Chapter 15. Captain Hausa. Bass Ass.

I took the two fugitives aft, and showed them their escape pod. The female, Maati, was almost vibrating with joy. It represented her route back home after all. Dr Dork Stratoe was ecstatic to see the plates that modify inertia. Poor chap, his papers had been ignored for so long, except by us of course.

I was just showing them around the cockpit when Mbeki ran over, and gasped that the radar showed jets and helicopters converging on us and we had, at best two minutes before they arrived.

Just then one of the jets buzzed us and the sonic boom sent the crew running. I muttered a few imprecations, virtually pushed the two guests into the pod and closed their hatch. Mbeki and I ran and dived over the side of the boat. We had a mini-sub, our escape route, anchored underneath the boat and we swam to it...

Chapter 16. Dork. Falling Up.

Seeing the inertial drive for the first time was like being re-introduced to a beloved son that you thought had died years earlier, but I did not have time to fully appreciate it. I had designed such a thing 15 years ago, and had been ridiculed for several years. Then just when I thought things couldn't get any worse, space travel became illegal, the ridicule stopped, and the harassment began. I had to promise never to work on my subject directly again. I have never understood why people are so threatened by new ideas. I've always loved them.

I didn't have much time for reflection though. Maati and I looked at each other in alarm as Captain Hausa slammed the hatch door shut.

"What do we do now?" said Maati.

On the control panel was taped a large sign saying "Press this."

I pressed it, and the ship began a power-up sequence as I watched marines climbing over the side of the boat out of the corner of my eye.

"Where did they come from?"
"I don't know, but I know where they are going!"

With a murderous look in her eyes Maati suddenly opened the

hatch again, pulled out a pistol and began shooting at the marines, who had not expected such a thing, and taken by surprise dived comically over the side of the boat again. She then closed the hatch quickly, and said sheepishly,

"Oops! I just remembered, we were supposed to keep the hatch closed!"

At that moment the wooden fishing boat exploded. From inside our spherical cocoon, which was metallic, dense and had a large inertial mass, the blast seemed mild, but the marines who were climbing back over the side were blown all over the place. We could see the remnants of the ship on fire for a few seconds through our windows, then my stomach leaped up through my throat as we dropped rapidly, and the light vanished from the windows.

"Who turned out the lights?" I said, holding onto a chair to avoid hitting the ceiling.
"We're underwater, Dork!" and so we were, rapidly falling.
"Some anti-gravity machine this is - we're sinking like a stone! Are all your theories as successful?" she asked, helpfully, quickly belting up and motioning for me to do the same.

At first we fell rapidly, but then we seemed to reach our buoyant level and bobbed there at some depth. I looked out of the windows at the teeming fish, silver-plated. They were used to the usual dark of the deep lake, and peered in puzzlement at the light streaming out of our windows.

“Fish! I don’t recognise the species – shame we can’t catch some!”
“No time.”

I flicked the switch to turn on the inertial drive I had been dreaming about all my life. I knew perfectly well how it worked. It was simply a smaller version of the experiment I’d done in my room nearly every night, to annoy my neighbour.

As I said earlier, the property we know as inertia is caused by a kind of radiation (Unruh radiation) that is only seen by bodies that accelerate and that is damped or reduced by the horizon that appears behind those objects as they accelerate. Imagine the Bad Ass at sea, surrounded by waves. They push on it from all directions equally. Now imagine that you suddenly, magically build a wall to the north of it. I have drawn it below. There will now be fewer waves to the north of the ship (the dark area) so it will be hit by more waves from the south and be pushed by them. The ship will move towards the wall (the horizon). Replace ocean waves with Unruh waves and you have a mechanism for inertial mass, or for making things move.

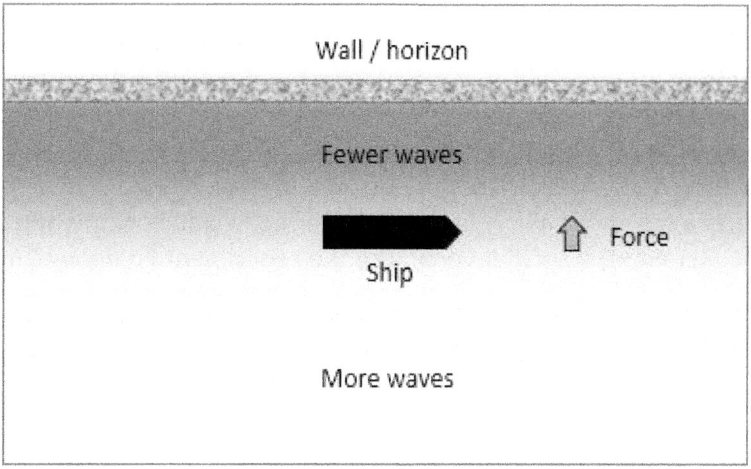

The crucial point for us is that if you use a conductive structure or plasma to interfere with these Unruh waves above the craft, you can damp them, and there will be more Unruh waves from below that will push it upwards. You can indeed modify inertia. Further, it is a gentle kind of thrust that doesn't throw you around the cabin – it works on the cabin and contents equally.

The upshot of all this theory is that we started moving slowly upwards. We did not feel the upwards acceleration but the spaceship began to judder, due to von Karman streets that were forming in the water beneath us as we moved up fast to the ocean surface. We broke the surface, smashing through the remains of the burning ship. There was a brief flash of fire at our windows and then an open, but grey sky, full of unfriendly black helicopters.

Looking out of the window, we were definitely accelerating but we could not feel it. I put on a seat belt anyway. I looked at the altimeter in some alarm, because so far we were rising by only about 10 metres per seconds, which was not fast enough to escape missiles.

"Can't this piece of junk go any faster?" said Maati, voicing my fears.
"We're accelerating. Cptn Hausa said it would be alright."
"That what's weird. We are accelerating but we can't feel it," said Maati.
"That's a horizon drive for you," I said.

I looked out of the window. We were still surrounded by a fleet of helicopters that were keeping up with our ascent. As a final touch, the marines inside them were waving at us. They must have been in good spirits since their target was such an easy one. One of them fired a missile at us, and it screamed towards us at a great rate leaving a trial of smoke.

"I love you," Maati said "but maybe you should have stayed on the ground."
"I love you too."
"Great," she said looking mournfully at the missile, "Do you think we'll make the papers?"
"Yes. Like Bonnie and Clyde. Don't worry about the missile, I have a hunch."

The missile was right outside our window, and we flinched ridiculously. Then almost comically, like someone being pulled up by one of Batman's contraptions, the missile was yanked upwards and out of sight.

"What happen to it?" said Maati in puzzlement.

I was joyfully in my element now.

"I knew it! It veered because when it got close, the inertial device in this ship changed its inertial mass and altered its trajectory upwards. It's being pulled up towards the same void in the vacuum (see the dark area in the picture) that is pulling us up. It's effectively an inertial shield!"

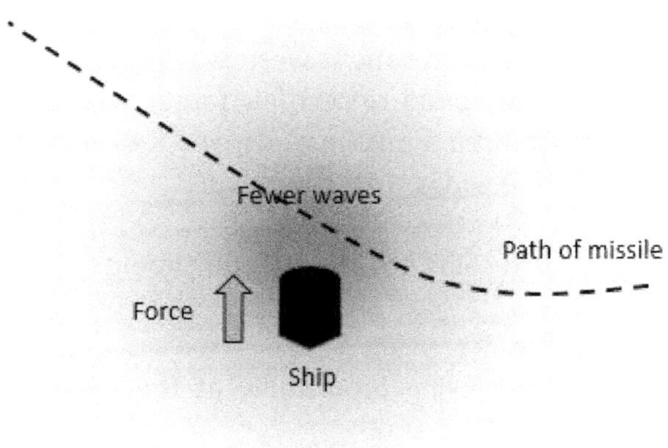

"So that's it! We're free?" said Maati.
"No. It will take us several hours for us to get into space at this rate. That is plenty of time for them to form a reception party and we're still vulnerable to weapons that have more speed than inertia. For example lasers. Let's hope your friends can get to us before they work that out."

Chapter 17. Yoder. A Needle in a Haystack.

I was in charge of the only space battle group that the Saturn colonies possessed. At that time we had no more than twelve frigates, each manned by between five and ten men. We had been ordered to Terra to rendezvous with a colonist, who amazingly, was said to be in the process of escaping from the planet. The Terrans were in pursuit. We had set out from the space station Kimiut. We had moved in towards Terra at one percent of the speed of light. Including acceleration and deceleration this had taken a few days and we had then formed up in the direction of the sun to avoid detection.

I led our flagship, the Qanik. Which housed 10 people. Myself and my second in command, a doctor, navigator, Casimeter operator (for detecting Unruh waves) and a few technical robots. The layout was quite similar to that of a boat for we all wore metal clothing and the floor was magnetised so there was a 'down'.

Our analysis of incoming Unruh waves had shown that there were several Terra ships pulling out of the Terra's gravitational well to engage us. We had had no word from the escaping colonist however, and I was becoming uneasy.

"There are twenty of them, Sir," said the Casimeter operator.
"What formation?"
"Widely spaced, but in cone formation: they know we are here,

Sir."
"The escape pod?"
"It is probably too small to be seen via Unruh waves, Sir."
"We need to know if the escapee is there, otherwise we're fighting pointlessly."
"Get in touch with them quick, or we'll have to break off."
"Yessir."

Chapter 18. Maati. Peril on the Karman Line.

We had been trying for several hours to operate the radio and either listen in or contact someone, and had failed. Dork was sat frowning at a piece of paper as he attempted to calculate what effect the inertial drive had on radio waves.

"We are now 100 km high. The border of space!" I said excitedly.

Dork looked up at me, without seeming to focus on me at all.

"Good, but damn, we can't radio out normally while the horizon drive is on. It interferes with the signal."

He dived back into his abstractions, and began looking at the ceiling and waving his fingers about. I tried again.

"Look. We could wait for ever for you to work that out. Why don't we simply turn off the horizon thingy for a bit, and then try to call someone?"

"What if we can't re-engage? We are not moving sideways fast enough to maintain an orbit around Terra by centrifugal forces. We may just drop out of the sky and burn up!"
"We've been rising up slowly for hours now, and my people will have sent some ships to intercept us. We have to make contact before they are attacked."

"OK. Damn. Do it. I can't calculate it, anyway, at the moment."
"I thought you invented this thing?"
"Yes, sort of, but I never thought I'd have to calculate the effect of inertial modification on radio waves in a hurry, while being suspended with no support 100 km above Terra in a claustrophobic pod with several hundred marines trying to kill me and an attractive woman sitting next to me. None of that helps concentration. And worse, I don't have my favourite type of blue pen!"

I turned off the horizon drive. Immediately we felt our stomachs churn as normal inertia and gravity came back and we began to descend. We'd been rising at 40 m/s, now we began to descend towards terminal velocity at 50 m/s.

"Oh. Good grief. Gravity's back in control," said Dork grabbing onto his seat, "Please make your call quick!"

I broadcast our position, and then Dork quickly turned the horizon drive back on. I remarked that we didn't appear to be going up again, and Dork explained that this was because the drive was only capable of accelerating us upwards slowly, and as we were descending at a terminal velocity of 50 or so metres per second it would take several minutes for us to start going up again.

Chapter 19. Yoder. Amman to the Rescue.

Tension was rising on the bridge, as the Terran ships had almost attained our altitude. Qaqasiut gave me a significant look.

“I think we’re going to have to run for it. There’s no one here to rescue, Sir.”

I glanced at Havela. Who shook his head.

“They must be there. Otherwise why the Terran fuss? Ee stay a bit longer.”
“May I remind you that in fifteen minutes they will be above us, and our tactical advantage will be lost, Sir,” said Qaqasiut.
“Let’s back out of the gravity well to remain above them.”

So, maintaining formation we slowly retreated up before the Terra ships.

Then Havela turned around and said:

“I have them! They just broadcast. Triangulating position now, Sir.”
“Good! What are the Terrans doing? Are they changing course?”
“Not yet.”
“Good. Send in the Amman.”
“Wait a moment,” said Qaqasiut. “What if they are using the

escape pod to draw us into battle? As soon as we look as if we have found them, they'll destroy the pod."
"That's why we're sending the little Amman in to rescue them."

So, as we backed up, drawing the Terra ships outward, the small Amman peeled off and dived to intercept the ascending escape ship, while we made preparations to attack.

Chapter 20. Brad Hambling. Cis-Terra defence.

At that time I was commanding the Cis-Terra defences of the UN. We'd been instructed to block the escape of a dangerous fugitive who apparently was trying to get information about Terra's defences to the rebels out in the colonies. The Outlander's ships were arranged above us, but fortunately had seemed up to this point too timid to attack even though they had the height advantage.

I was stood on the bridge of our flagship, sipping coffee, when our grav-op motioned to me to come over.

"Sir. They're moving in to attack." He looked at me white faced.
"Good. I'm tired of all this cat and mouse. Signal the other ships to move into battle positions."

I gulped my coffee, and sat down in the command chair. I had faced battle situations in simulations before, never in real space. We'd never had an opposition before! Projected before me was a hologram showing the arrangement of our ships in white and the Outlanders in bright red. They had looked like two cones facing each other: > < but slowly as I watched both changed shape in preparation for the battle tending towards a flat-fronted shape: | |.

My second in command, Michel Ney, arrived on the bridge, alerted to the crisis. He was still putting on his environment suit as he began to talk.

"They must have located the bait," he said.
"I'm surprised it has taken so long. Anyway, the strategists on Terra were right, we've managed to use the escapee to bring the colonials fleet out into the open for a straight battle. If we can finish the bulk of their ships here we might stand a chance of destroying their colonies."
"Something to tell the grandchildren isn't it? We'll have cleared the Sol system of pirates."
"Order Goldhardt on the Prism to destroy the escaping pod."
"Yessir."

Chapter 21. Dork. Shotgun Marriage.

We'd managed to begin rising again, but I'd bitten my nails to shreds. The space craft we could now see out of the window were keeping pace with us. They were a menacing presence. We'd managed to pass the time talking, but eventually a silence had crept over us. Maati was the first to say what was bothering us both.

"Why isn't that ship firing on us? We're bait?"
"The UN have being trying to bring your fleet to an open battle for years. I don't want to think about it."
"But we must. There must be something we can do!"
"Probably not. Once they have your fleet, they'll fire on us."

I was looking out of the window at the bright blue curve of Terra. We were moving upwards at the equator and also slightly westwards because of our changed inertial mass, and so the sun was about to rise in the west. The horizon was already glowing, when a searing blaze of light erupted from a point near the equator and obscured everything else. The cockpit was bathed in brilliant light and, used to near darkness, we both had to cover our eyes.

Then oddly there were some milder flashes of light in the other window. I looked, passed Maati, and it seemed one of the ships that had been shadowing us for hours was ablaze. It slowly turned towards us and fired and I thought it had decided to finish us, but, it seemed, they were firing past us at someone. I looked back out the other window towards the sun and could just about make out a dark shape moving near the sun, growing in size.

"What are you doing?" said Maati, "watching a tennis match?"
"Yes, a deadly one," I said, smiling. "Your friends are here, look!"
Maati peered out of her window at the burning ship. It was still on fire, and was now sinking relative to us, as its primitive reaction drive must have been knocked out. Maati turned a 100 watt grin on me.
"Piajuq!"
I assumed by her tone of voice that was something like "Fantastic!"

However, the Terra ship was still bravely firing, luckily past us, at the other oncoming ship. Then they seemed to realise that, as they were falling, and we were rising, we would soon ascend out of range of them, and maybe an order had come through for our destruction. Anyway, they began firing at us, with a smaller plasma gun on their upper side.

"Clever guys." I said.

Huge spheres of plasma passed us by, one that passed very close shorted all the instruments on our control panel and soon the cockpit was filled with smoke. Then our stomach leaped up into our throats as we began, once again, to fall out of the sky, following the Terran ship which was still firing up at us, falling down to a fiery death.

"Can't your friends throw us a grappling hook or something?" I suggested.
"They can do better than that! They'll have a tractor beam on us soon."
"A tractor beam? That sounds like something out of Star Trek."
"We have made some advances. You'll see."

A minute later I was still waiting, biting my nails, watching the developing red tinge outside the window, and beginning to feel the heat as our pod warmed up as a prelude to burning up. Maati was frantically jabbering in Inuit on the radio. She gave up, and slammed the mike down on the control panel. She pointed her face at the ceiling and screamed unreservedly.

"Scheisse! They seem to have had a malfunction with the magnet beam," she said, looking me in the eye with a desperate-knowing look.
"That did not sound like Inuit."
"We use Penn Dutch to swear in. More effective somehow."
"The ground is getting bigger out there!" I said looking out of the window.
"And it's getting hot in here," she said taking of her jumper.

"Do you have marriage in your colonies?" I said, looking at her.
"Yes, of course!" she said.
"Well, I'd like to marry you then."

"It's easy to say that isn't it... just before you die! You get all the impact and none of the responsibility."
"I promise, if we ever survive this, to marry you."
"Offer accepted," she said.

Just then, there was tremendous jolt and the pod started spinning slowly, but our downward spiral had stopped.

"They seem to have repaired the magnet beam," she said.
"You orchestrated that very well. Now I've just promised my life to you," I said with mock anger, and sincere relief.

In that new dawn of life we embraced, and did the normal romantic, things, as we were dragged upwards in the tractor beam to rendezvous with the colonists' ship. I was ecstatically happy, because I seemed to have achieved everything I had ever wanted. A beautiful woman, fulfilment of my technical dreams, freedom and space travel despite myself. But such things are never so lightly given.

Chapter 22. Yoder. Sprites.

We knew, right from the start, that we couldn't hope to win a pitched battle. The opposition was too strong. The population, and productivity of Terra was still huge even with the wrecked climate, some 1 billion people with well established industries, whereas our colonies were new and housed only about 30,000 people with a severely limited set of resources.

Our attack was really a feint. Our twelve ships aimed straight for the heart of their flotilla, firing as we went. The UN ships' defence shields deflected all of our plasma weapons, which was slightly unnerving. Their 25 ships parted to let us pass through, which we did quickly.

However, we had an ally that the Terrans knew nothing about. In the atmosphere of Saturn there are lightning strikes thousands of times larger than those on Terra and a flying life-form has evolved that, for want of a better phrase, eats electricity. These organisms, 'sprites' we called them, loved to cling to electrical circuitry and extract electricity from ships. Several of our ships that had ventured into the gas giant in the early days had disappeared without a trace. As we found out later, they had been sucked dry by Sprites.

As we passed through their fleet, we fired several Sprites at them. They drifted around in open space for a few seconds, then, unable to believe their luck they began to home in on the

Terran ships for an early lunch.

Things were beginning to go badly for us, however, as the Terran ships opened fire with some huge plasma guns. We'd not seen their like before, and the Nikolai, one of our ships and its crew of five was vapourised instantly by one of these plasma shells. Its shields had had no effect at all! Everyone on the bridge looked at me, as news came in of the loss, as if they expected me somehow to call off the attack, but we had to wait until the Amman with its precious cargo had caught up with us.

Then a cheer went up on the bridge, as one of the Terran ships began to glow, a sign that a Sprite had attached itself to it, and was having a feast. At the conference before we left Saturn's orbit we had agreed on this method of fighting, because, although slightly messy, it was reasonably moral, because the crew of the ships was not usually killed. The human body is mostly water which protects it from the creatures. The ships, although unable to fight, were still habitable when the life support systems came back. The attacks were short enough that the Terran ships may not even have had time to fall out of the sky.

Havela, our communicator, turned to me and informed me that the Amman was converging on our party.

"How long till they get here?"
"Two minutes, Sir."
"Have they picked up any hostile followers?"

"No."
"That calls for a beer! Let's go home!"

Chapter 23. Dork. On the Amman.

I was so relieved that the Amman had us, that I didn't for a moment mind the fact that our escape pod was spinning madly. Suddenly, just when I felt I was about to be sick, there was an abrupt jerk, we stopped spinning and a bright light appeared through the pod window.

"I think we are aboard," said Maati with a gleeful grin.
"Let's hope they don't mind having a Terran aboard," I said, with some trepidation. I had heard that colonists had a fanatical hatred of Terrans.

Then the pod door was flung open, and a wide Russian-style face looked in.

"Dva?!" the face said in some surprise. This means "two" in Russian.

Maati launched into an animated conversation with the fellow, in what indeed sounded like Russian. He eventually held up his hands as if in despair, a gesture common to men of most cultures, and motioned for us to get out of the pod.

I had been strapped down, but now I stood up and I was weightless. It was disorienting. Which way was down? Luckily, I decided for myself which way was down based on what the crew were stood on, and that helped. Maati got out first, and then I ventured out too. The spacecraft looked similar to films I had seen of submarines from the 20th Century. The walls were metallic, the smell was metallic, and this fitted in well with the language. Russian, though to me one of the most beautiful languages, had always seemed a little metallic.

There were three people there to greet us, and they didn't seem to be pleased to see us at all. Maati whispered sideways at me.

"These are Russians. We Inuit colonists tend to have different colonies to the Russians. The Amish also live separately. Though we fight together against the Terrans, we don't always get along very well."
"Wonderful," I said. "They don't want to send us back?"
"No. Don't worry. The captain will treat us well, I'm sure."

We were both floating in the air, while the crew, somehow, were rooted to the ground. The mystery was solved when they offered us metal overalls and Maati explained the idea behind magnetic suits. I put on one and enjoyed a very welcome attraction to the floor. The crew all motioned to us hurriedly to go forward onto the bridge.

"Maati," said a deep voice. And Maati launched herself at a big bear like man, causing me a little concern.
"Vulpis! I wondered if you'd be here. Is Morley with you?"
"Yes. He's on the floor over there, switched off, otherwise he'd give us more stress then the battle!"

Maati returned and dragged me onto the bridge, said

"This is Dr Vulpis. He was my favourite teacher at school. He used to give us virtual lessons from one of the more remote colonies."
"How are you Maati? All right? Hope these Terrans haven't damaged you?"
"No, though they have done their best. Except Dork here, of course."
Vulpis turned his attention to me.
"You are to be thanked, sir!"

I didn't know what to say and tried to change the subject.

"Why is this ship called the Amman?"
"Ah. Good question. The man who founded the Amish church, Mr Amman, once escaped from a prison. His guard chased him but fell into a freezing lake. Amman went back to rescue him, and was arrested and then executed."
"Seems a little unfair."
"A little?"
"You're a professor? What subject do you teach?"
"Literature."
"They stopped teaching that a long time ago."
"It figures. I bet they banned this one: 'We here highly resolve that these dead shall not have died in vain—that this nation, under God, shall have a new birth of freedom—and that government of the people, by the people, for the people, shall

not perish from the Earth'."
"I've not heard it before. A lot of literature was lost in The Crustal Shift."
"That was Abraham Lincoln."
"Who?"
"You'll learn. We've preserved a lot you may not have seen. We believe the UN deleted possibly 80% of literature and 90% of films for the public's safety."

One of the crew interrupted.

"Vulpis! We have company, save the literature for later!"
"Alright. Let's get going...you two, strap yourselves in!"

We were pushed into seats and strapped ourselves in. There was a sudden forward acceleration, followed by a vibration, as we were pulled up out of Terra's atmosphere.

"Where are you from?" said Vulpis.
"New Cambridge."
"I'm impressed."
"Don't be," I said. "It's not like the old one. Clever but not curious. Not creative anymore."

A blue flash outside the front cockpit windows momentarily blinded us, and a blue shimmering spread along the cockpit walls and dissipated at the back.

"That was close," said a crewmember who I later found out was called Vlad. He turned around and winked at me "Another inch, and Valhalla!"

"I'm fed up with these Terrans. Let's turn around and face them," said Vulpis.

We did. I felt the acceleration, and could see the Terran ships in the window as we headed for them.

"They are cowards. We'll make as if to ram them and they'll pull aside. It'll rattle them."

The enemy ship grew rapidly in the window, and I looked at Maati.

"Are all your countrymen as mad as this?" I said with some concern.

The ruse worked. The Terran ships panicked, stopped firing and moved in a panic out of our way. The crew were intent on firing, but Vulpis said no.

"We haven't to give them an excuse to follow us home. We have to play fair, then they will leave us alone."

I felt this to be decent, but naive, and said so. Vulpis replied.

"Sometimes you just have to gamble on human nature."

We accelerated out towards the rest of the colonists' fleet, into space, leaving the Terran ships, rattled, but alive.

"Vlad. Call Yoder and tell him the seaweed's in the bag."

Chapter 24. Yoder. Running.

Our plan was clear. Rescue Maati. From a moral standpoint it was necessary, and also, she had been on Terra – an instant spy. However, we worried that the Terrans might follow us back to the colonies, and for this reason we were being careful not to destroy any of their ships. Hence the use of Sprites.

If this policy failed and the Terrans did follow us home, then we would have to retreat into the infinite open space that we had at our disposal, drawing the enemy on towards us, away from his supply lines, and rely also on his inexperience in deep space. The sort of Russian strategy that had broken a namesake of mine a long time ago.

As soon as we heard that the Amman had picked up our escapees we turned and ran. Not a very honourable thing to do, but when you are outnumbered, there is a certain wisdom in it.

Chapter 25. Hambling. Qualms.

The night after the battle, I sat alone in my cabin with a glass of Equadorian wine. The only kind of wine left, except in the cellars of the super-rich. The floor of my room was made of very thick glass, through which I could see Terra, as it rotated slowly beneath us. I watched my ice-bound ethnic home state: Quebec rise over the horizon. Since the spin axis was now in Greenland, also hidden under ice, Quebec was a place where the night and days lasted half the year. Quebecois like me were linked to that place only by culture. The Inuit had colonised it though, as they had most of the planet – but they were thinly scattered. I wondered why it was that these colonists, who we had been told were little more than mutated animals, with no morals, had suffered casualties themselves, but had ensured that none of our people were killed.

I held my glass of wine in my hand, against the light, watching it become blood red, as if illuminated from within. We should have lost the battle. Their use of an organism to disable my ships had left us almost defenceless, but they had not capitalised on that, and had merely disappeared, back to Saturn, taking the dangerous organism with them. Foolish, or noble?

Wine was a cushion to avoid painful thoughts because of the orders I had received:

"Pursue the rebels to Saturn, destroy their bases, and take their

populations captive. Fifteen more battle cruisers, and 26 supply ships are being sent to you.
We're also sending up a political officer."

Great..

Chapter 26. Dork. Dork Meets Morley.

The Amman, the small spaceship we were on, had rejoined the fleet, and we could see the other ships out of the windows. I stared at them in amazement, with my arm around Maati's neck, and for the first time since I was young, I felt possibilities expand. I could go anywhere, say anything, and there would be little to pay in return.

The merry-faced Vulpis surged out of the cockpit, passing us by saying:

"Hey Kids, get yourselves strapped in. We have to leave fast!"

I looked at Maati:

"What's all that about?"
"There are things you Terrans don't know about. Solar waves for example."
"Solar waves? You mean the Solar wind?"
"You'll have to ask Vulpis for the details. I'm just a humble hydroponic farmer, but the gist of it is that we hitch a ride on particles streaming from the sun. Vulpis, I assume is going to the back of the ship to watch the spectacle."

This, I wanted to see, so I hurried after him. I found him staring at a visual display, and occasionally out of the window at the other ships of our convoy. He grinned round at me in his half-mad way.

“It will be a good show. Look especially at the other ships, as the wave approaches us they will switch on their “wings” on by one, and accelerate away from us. We’ll be one of the last to leave.”
“Why?”
“Because our wings won’t deploy. I’ll have to get Morley to fix them.”

With that he kicked what appeared to be a small dustbin on the floor, which immediately darted up into the air, sprouted arms and legs and hovered like a dark tinkerbell, lights flashing.

“Morley! Solar wings not open. Fix electro connect A7-33,” said Vulpis.
“OK. Me do!” said the strange contraption. It zoomed off, slamming into the wall.
“Morley! Wait,” said Vulpis, and looked at me exasperated:
“Morley is a wizz at electronics, not so good at mundane things!”

A small airlock opened in the wall, and Morley plunged into it. The door closed again.

“He plays chess too. He’s good.”
“We have robots on Terra. They seem more reliable that that one. Sorry,” I said, “I didn’t mean to be offensive.”
“Please, be offense! We like a bit of offense up here. Livens things up.”

Suddenly Morley appeared at the window, just as if he was peering in, then he slowly sank below the bottom of the window frame, disappeared for a few moments, then zoomed upwards into view again. Vulpis laughed.

"He's a real comedian is Morley. Did you see that? The difference with our robots is that, unlike yours now, which are programmed by a human and do not develop, we still have some that used the old methods. They are grown from digital seeds in a virtual reality, so that they have personalities. This means that, although they are eccentric, they have more flexible problem-solving skills."

"You mean they have artificial intelligence?"

"Yes. I suppose you could say that. Ah, he's done it!"

I looked out of the window to see huge blue shimmering wings covered with laminar plasma spreading out. Slowly they curved forwards, pushed by the weak but steady flow from the sun of electrons and protons. Our ship began to accelerate out into deep space. I could see most of the blue armada out of the window. Like the sailing ships of old but made of light and in three dimensions.

Morley re-appeared in the airlock, and banged on the door a few times while Vulpis struggled to open it.

"Morley! Patience!" he said.

When the door was open, Morley roared out of it for a couple of feet towards me, then remained static.

"He's inspecting you," said Vulpis.

The little robot angled himself so that he was five degrees off horizontal. Unconsciously, I must have mimicked him, angling my head slightly on one side. This seemed to please him as he began zooming round the room.

"For crying out loud," said Vulpis, "Morley! Off!"

Immediately Morley switched off and his inert body crashed to the ground.

"That's a bit cruel isn't it?"
"Yes. Aber es muss sein."
"Is that a quote from Beethoven?"
"Yes, but I meant it also. He gets on my nerves sometimes."

Chapter 27. Hambling. Reluctance.

That night I had retired to my cabin, and was listening the Dire Straits', Love over Gold in the dark. One of the few groups from the 1980s still allowed – as they were apolitical. I was listening to: Telegraph Road, in which Mark Knopfler describes the evolution of a few scattered people into a society, which then gets tied up into knots. That song had always impressed me.

A holographic symbol representing 'someone calling' appeared next to my head, and I reached out and touched it to signal that I would receive the call. Dire Straits ceased in mid-riff. Cmdr Guiy, the political officer who had recently slithered up from Terra, suddenly appeared as a blue-ish hologram beside my couch. A perfect face, but cold eyes.

"Well, General. It looks as if the mutants are going home."
"Yes. I know it," I said. "They are based at the old water mining sites."
"That is what the boffins say. Time to eliminate them."
"Have you considered negotiating? Save a few lives?"
"No. They are uncontrollable – an unpredictable factor."
"Appoint a governor then?"
"They are too far away. Impossible to enforce compliance."

Guiy's image flickered slightly and the ghost-like face frowned.

"General. You are with us aren't you?"

“They showed chivalry in the recent battle.”
“We have faith in you General. The Terran Order expects much from you. These animals must be destroyed before they become strong enough to destroy us. If you are not with us.”
“I will not let the Terran Order down.”
“Wise. Live in the Order.”

The hologram disappeared leaving blackness. I had formerly agreed with everything Guiy had said. The number of atrocities committed by the rebels over the years did not bear counting. I had seen, on the news, pictures of towns burnt by them, and heard the testimony of women raped, children gassed. I had hated them for years, and a few weeks ago I would have been looking forward to exacting retribution.

Yet, during the recent battle they had had me by the hair, and had not pulled. Why? Stupid or noble? Could it be that I had been fed false information? Anyway, despite my confusion, it was clear that disobedience meant death. Besides, my government, the only viable one on Terra, which had been so good to me all these years could not be wrong, could it?

Chapter 28. Maati. The Trek Home.

It took us nine days to pass safely through the asteroid belt and make the rest of the trip to Saturn. Dork was like a schoolboy, and spent almost the entire time staring out of the window, watching with rapt awe as dull grey asteroids drifted past and watching the ringed planet become larger. The rest of the time he spent watching, Star Wars, which he apparently had never heard of before.

The time was exciting for me as well. I would soon see my parents again, not my sister, but at least I could talk about her and lay her to rest. She was gone and it was as if the island I lived on had suddenly become much smaller and less interesting. The bell had tolled for me, as Hemingway would say. No longer would she regale me excitedly with tales of her blossoming romances. She had been my main confidante. Now, who would I talk to? Dork reckoned I could talk to him, and this was true, but men are not the same, and there would always be things I could not say, things I know he would never understand.

Chapter 29. Dork. Films!

In my parents' home in my birth city Lovelock, when the sky had been clear, I had often used my telescope, a three-inch refractor, to look at Saturn, the most beautiful of the planets. The most fascinating was Jupiter because of the Galileian moons, four of them, that moved around the planet. You could see night after night that they had moved, and share Galileo's excitement when they suggested to him the idea that the planets, including Terra he was stood upon, actually rotated around the Sun in the same way. Regarded as a heretic, but he was just trusting his eyes.

As we approached Saturn, I discovered the most amazing film called Star Wars in their archives. I watched it in awe. A single person, took on a massive empire and defeated it. I'd never seen a film like it before, but Maati said most of them were actually like that, but the Terran government must have deleted them all. I didn't believe her, so I picked another at random called Local Hero. That was the same! All the films I'd seen were about an individuals' acceptance of the status quo and how that brings its own rewards.

I sat almost all day by the windows of our ship watching these amazing films and the approaching planet, and the occasional asteroid that passed us by. I also tried to learn Inuit from a tablet I'd been given. Maati often sat next to me, reading another tablet in silence, going through my Inuit with me, or teasing me sexually, by tossing her hair back to reveal her curved shirt front.

Eventually I could see Saturn with the naked eye, and then the banded clouds became visible. Then the swirls and eddies in the clouds, each one bigger than Terra. Finally we approached Enceladus, a white cracked world surrounded by what appeared to be many tinier moons, which turned out to be manmade.

We approached one of them, Maati's home, Iqaluit. It was perhaps a 500 metres in diameter, and looked rather like a collection of old beer bottles that had been glued together to form a wagon wheel shape. Maati explained:

"It has a modular design, you see? If the station is attacked the individual components can separate and scatter."

It was still disturbing to me to hear that Terra had attacked the colonies so often. The media had not mentioned that. Slowly we approached Iqaluit, having folded our Solar wings, accompanied by the rest of the fleet, and entered a large hanger that had been formed from the axial bottle. The entrance to this seemed to be protected by a force field that glowed a deep blue, and probably sealed the atmosphere inside. Inside the hanger waited crowds of people. There were some raised areas and we landed on one of those. Would I be welcomed or lynched?

Chapter 30. Maati. Home at Last.

I was excited to be home! Of course the hanger was very familiar to me since I'd often been there with schoolmates to cheer the intrepid crew of one of our jerry-built ships as it set off to form another colony. To us, it was always particularly sad to see the young men that we knew, often handsome, enter the ship and think that we would never, or rarely, see them again.

Speaking to the station before we had docked on the radio we had expressed concerns about the likely reaction to Dork's arrival. Since the recent raids from Terra, passions had been aroused. Our mayor, Dr Vladim Iqaavom, had agreed to give a welcome speech explaining how Dork had saved the day.

I retrieved the bottle of dirty lake water from the Amman. Gave it to our Chief of Hydroponics who exclaimed loudly and dashed off to his labs to analyse it.

Chapter 31. Dork. Iqaluit.

For the last two days my Inuit had advanced by leaps and bounds. I had also studied some of the colony's history. The tablet projected the information onto the ship's gun-metal wall. Neat device. It seems the lack of space in the colonies had encouraged miniaturisation. The Inuit colony had originally been a water mining station, with a largely Inuit population. In the original settlement by mining companies, the Inuit had been chosen because of their ability to live in extremely cold environments and because of their practicality. The Amish had later been sent out to run farms with the extracted water. During the global crisis, groups of escaping Europeans, Russian and Chinese joined them, but the Inuit and Amish were still in a majority and their languages were the ones generally used.

Docking was interesting because the station was spinning, presumably to use centrifugal force to replace gravity, so the entry hangar was at the north pole of the station. After landing, Vardis opened the door, with a bang, there was gust of wind as the air pressure was equalised with the station, and we all trooped out into a surprisingly dim light. Perhaps it was comfortable for Inuit so far from the Sun.

The station was disorienting at first because the floors were not magnetically induced, but were induced by the outwards centrifugal force from the station's spin. So when we left the ship, which was parked on the axis of the central cylinder, we had to push off and drift slowly to the concave outside wall of the cylinder which was the floor, and where everyone was standing. As we did so the 'gravity' increased till eventually the mind decided that, yes, the outside shell of the cylinder was the floor and we ended up falling down onto it.

As we landed, a great cheer went up, and suddenly we were surrounded by a chaotic melee of people. The men shaking hands with us. The women kissing us on both cheeks. Oddly they addressed me in Pennsylvania Dutch, probably thinking I was Amish. Then the mayor, appeared, a jolly individual. His importance solely demonstrated by a small microphone next to his mouth. He looked quite informal and relaxed, as he greeted all the crew in turn.

When he got to me he held his hand to his ear, as if listening to an ear-piece, then switched to English.

"Ah. Dr Dork Stratoe I presume. Welcome to Iqaluit!"
"Thank you. I'm glad to be here in peace and in one piece."

He shook my hand, to my obvious relief, then said in a low voice.

"We're having a meeting tonight to discuss policy regarding the approach of the Terran ships. I'd like you to be there, since you know about the psychology of Terrans. Maati is going also. She'll guide you to the right place."

I was surprised by this. Surely it must have occurred to them that I might be a spy, sent ahead to gather information about their possible defence policy.

"Thanks. I'm honoured you trust me."
"Maati trusts you, and we trust her judgement."

He leaned closer.

"Betray us though, and we'll put you off onto Enceladus's ice." He winked.

Chapter 32. Dork. Council meeting.

I should have been preparing for the meeting, but in fact I spent the time searching the archives for more films. I found The Name of the Rose, and again, the same theme: one man defeats an empire, and saves a few books in the process. I was still reeling when I walked into the war council meeting with Maati. In most of the station the gravity was imposed magnetically, so once again we were wearing iron clothing. The, mostly, elderly men sat around the table, looked as though they had a huge weight hanging from their chins, such were their long faces.

The most hairy of the men, a Russian wearing a red armband and identified by his name tag as Janov, stood up, and a holographic projection appeared over the table showing Enceladus, the Space Stations orbiting it, the few friendly vessels defending it and, further out, a massed armada of hostiles from the mother planet, come to stamp out their offspring. The old Greek legend about Saturn eating his children did occur to me, but it was Terra doing it, not Saturn.

“Well,” he said. “We have a problem. The enemy have 52 ships, to our 15, and refuse to negotiate. They intend, they say, to take us back to Terra. We need ideas, so I invite the representative of each racial grouping to stand up and present his peoples’ opinion of what we should do.”

He said it in Russian of course, but it was translated into English by the eccentric robot Morley, who hovered next to me, wobbling about, broadcasting the translation into a receptor near my ear.

The head of the Russian delegation stood up.

"We should evacuate Saturn orbit, and head outwards to Neptune. We know how to extract fuel and food from the environment out here. The Terrans don't. They may therefore run out of supplies, and return to Terra."

The head of the German group stood up,

"We believe that although our ships are fewer than theirs, we have a secret weapon, the Sprites, and we have far more experience in space. I vote we stay and fight."

The head of the Chinese group then stood up, but at that point Morley went into one of his abstract dances and all I understood was that they were suggesting a complicated deception using holographic decoys, which sounded a little outlandish at this late stage.

All eyes then turned on me. Janov stood, and to my amusement, and embarrassment, invited me to speak for the English racial group, of which I was the only member. I stood up, I had formulated an idea on the Amman, and discussed it with Maati.

"Well, of course, you should regard my words as less informed as I do not know the layout out here. All I would say is that the Terran government is not a moral one. They mean to destroy you. Taking each idea in turn. The Russian idea of retreat, would be difficult, because we are already as good as surrounded. Some may escape, but only some. You have a whole community that is threatened, women and children too. All the Terra ships have to do is seek them out and hold them hostage."

Janov:

"Alright. You've told us what not to do. What should we do. You know the mentality of Terrans. We know nothing of it. What would you do?"

"You have no hope of victory over their armada. However, you have a chance of victory over their minds. The regime on Terra is unpopular. Even the soldiers and generals that serve it, do it only because there is no alternative for advancement. Why not try to convince the attacking fleet to mutiny?"
"And how can we do that?" said a burly Russian in a low sarcastic voice, "Maybe we should offer them a lifetime supply of seaweed?"

A ripple of grim laughter went round the table.

"There are many examples of invaders pulling back because of unexpected feelings of morality. The German general occupying Rome in the Second World War, refused an order to fortify the city and defend it, thus saving the city a destructive siege because he thought it was a treasure of mankind and should be preserved. Also, the Russian invaders of Britain, during the early stages of the Post-Shift Wars, allowed an area in the southeast that included London, Oxford and Cambridge to remain undamaged and independent, to avoid destroying the unique culture therein – which was destroyed eventually by the ice anyway. This space community you have built, is unique, and a treasure of mankind. I can't believe than rank and file Terrans want to destroy it."

One of the Chinese delegation stood up, and shook his head thoughtfully.

"You're a naive idealist. I cannot imagine these attackers care about things like human treasures. They will be mostly conscripts who are likely to blame us for the danger they find themselves in."

This was indeed the sentiment around the table, and the debate began to favour the Russian idea of withdrawal to Neptune, but I noticed Janov occasionally looked at me thoughtfully.

At the end of the meeting, when the groups had drifted off by themselves for further debate Janov walked over to Maati and I, and sat on the table next to us.

"I liked what you said. I don't believe it will work, but maybe some Terrans are not so bad after all."

"The people are fine, just lied to."
"Do you believe in your idea enough to try it out?" he said.
"Me?"
"Yes, of course. You're from Terra, you'll be able to infiltrate them better than any of us."
"...and do what exactly?" I interrupted.
"Cause them to mutiny."

I was going to laugh, but that was exactly what I had been suggesting. In theory, it had seemed fine. When faced with the practicalities it seemed ridiculous.

"Think about it," said Janov sympathetically.
"Come on," said Maati encouragingly. "Let's go see Kudravtsev!"

Chapter 33. Dork. Kudravtsev.

Apparently, since he was older and preferred a lower gravity, the "Professor" lived in one of the boxes near the rotational centre of the station. He was the engineer responsible for the Great Trek into space. As I stood there with Maati and Morley he opened his door, glared very effectively at me, without seeing Maati at all. He was a typical Russian with a strong, broad, pale face, now lined and then with age and crowned with wisps of white hair.

"Go away! You're interrupting me!! I have very important meeting!"

He slammed the door violently in my face and, since the gravity was low the floor-tremor bounced me quite effectively upwards. I came back down slowly unsure what to do next. Maati, gave me a sideways glance, and knocked again

"You'll have to excuse the Prof. I'm sure the reason he doesn't want to meet us is that he's preparing to meet us. Take it as a compliment."

The door opened again

"Pest! Now..."

His mouth fell open.

"Maati! I'm so sorry, I didn't..".

He burst into tears when she moved forwards to hug him. Eventually he forced himself to stop blubbering.

"You know a while back I thought those Terrans had done for you."
"No Kay, they haven't succeeded yet. As you probably know, Dork here engineered my escape, and he's going to regret it for the rest of his life!"

K slowly focussed on me, clearly he'd heard the whole thing already.

"Young man, you must be thanked, and.." he grinned, ".. also commiserated. If you wanted a quiet life, you better go deaf!"

He held out his hand for me to shake, while Maati bit her lip in indignation.

"Getting of the planet these days is difficult isn't it? You may know that we had some trouble ourselves back in my day."
"Well, the Great Trek is not in the history books, but I read about it elsewhere."
"Really? Under which heading? Crimes of the Century?"
"Yes, I think so! But everyone reads the story..."

"Bah! Story! It's true - better than a story...and call me K."

We entered his room, which was decorated with pine-wood parquet floors, and pine furniture. “Pine. My last piece of Russia!” he said, as I knelt down and touched it. The soft hue and smell of wood was a soothing relief after all the sterile white corridor I’d seen. I sat down rather quickly on one of the chairs in the room. It was like lying down on a water-bed, as my movement set the chair oscillating. I stood up again and bent down to see what sort of suspension the chair had. There was nothing between it and the ground! K was looking at me with a playful expression.

“I was wondering if you’d notice. There’s a weak horizon drive in the chair.”
“I guessed that,” I said. “Nothing doing!”
“Indeed,” he said. “The very real pull of the non-existent vacuum”
“What we thought was nothing a long time ago.”
“I know some of the theory, “ said K, “but I have not read your later papers on enhancing it because they were classified. So, we have one or two horizon drives but very weak and only for gimmicks like this.”
“Like my namesake and hero, Strato of Lampsacus. He was the last true ancient Greek physicist and his work made possible real steam engines. He could have started the industrial revolution before the time of Christ, but confined himself to building marvels for the temples.”

Maati was enjoying the debate.

"Well, I'll just leave you physicists alone," she said, pleased that we were getting along.
"Now K likes tea, being Russian. How about you Dork? You are English aren't you?"
"Yes. I am. You have tea?"

K was indignant.

"I'm Russian. Of course we have tea! We brought some from Terra, like many other things. The Amish can grow anything in their hothouses."

He settled down slowly on his sofa.

"So, we have heard something about you all these years. We pick up TV broadcasts from Terra and I was interested in your experiments, when of course they were briefly broadcast 20 years ago."
"Oh, you saw that broadcast? Ha. I think more people saw it off planet than on. On Terra people seem more interested in immersing themselves in pleasing virtual realities, than trying to learn about the real world."
"Ha! Why study for the exam, if you can pretend you're already passed it. I can sympathise with that. I was not good at exams. I hated having to learn to do things the way others had already done them. I always wanted to do things in new way, and so make them mine."

Maati came with our drinks, and sat down, looking at us in turn. K sipped his black tea – who drinks black tea? - said

"What do you think of the colonies?"
"Glorious so far."
"Why?"
"I feel I can say anything."
"I suppose you can, but they won't let you do everything."

Maati giggled to herself.

"Oh, K.. Just because they don't want to go to Proxima like you do."
"Maybe the Terrans will force our hand."
"K!"
"Have you heard of Hermann Hesse? No, probably not, he was one of many German philosophers. Terra may have censored his writings now, but he said: "The egg is the world. To be born we must destroy a world." To progress you must first destroy your familiar environment, but this destruction will force you to design a new, hopefully better, one."

"The new state could be worse," I said, naturally adopting the stance of devil's advocate. "For instance, how about the communist revolution!"

"Well, it's all well and good to criticize it now, but it achieved the industrialisation of Russia efficiently and just in time to counter the German invasion. Later on huge crimes and problems came to the fore, but it wasn't all bad. Also, the communist revolution was in some ways a splendid example for all mankind not to follow. It was a necessary experiment. Now we know that communism is unpleasant, but we know that only because some people tried it! If we didn't know that we might waste energy now by trying it. Fascism too was a useful experiment. Everything that is half-sensible must be tried so that the best can be chosen, just as in a debate all suggestions must be heard and seriously considered. This is the way evolution works too with its random mutations."

What he was suggesting seemed to me to be a recipe for a fractious, war-torn world, and I pointed this out to him, but he began again.

"You are correct. All the most creative societies in history have also been the most violent. Look at medieval Italy which combined Leonardo da Vinci with his heightened sensibilities and the Borgia who used to lock people up in cages hung from towers in public. Or early 20th Century Germany which produced the genius of Einstein and Von Braun, but then invaded almost everyone."

"So, what are you saying? Injustice and cruelty are necessary?"

"Look at Terra. It now enjoys peace, but it is the peace of the graveyard because no-one can oppose authority. Total order. There is no debate, or experiment. Disagreement, conflict, and pain, are necessary for progress."

"I think there has to be a balance between order and chaos." Said Maati quietly.
"Well, you would." Said K, amused.
"What do you mean by that?"
"Look up the ancient Egyptian Gods sometime! The God Maati had the job of making sure there was the right balance of order and chaos. She was married to the God Thoth as well, who was sort of a scientist." He looked at us both "History rhymes."

"I always assumed that we always move forward linearly."
"Don't be so sure. You know we found inscriptions on Mars?"
"Inscriptions?"
"Yes, we were prospecting for silicon there. It's rich in it. They found an underground bunker and dated it to 10,000 BC."
"You're saying cave men went to Mars?"
"You find it hard to accept? Even you, after a lifetime of scepticism."
"Sorry. You're right. One should never dismiss data, no matter how odd."

K beamed.

"I knew you were good! That's the basis of science right there!"

"Thank you. But getting back to your pain is progress. It seems to me that the pain you mention is real and measurable, but the progress is not easily measured. How can you be sure that the overall balance is positive?"

"Is progress good? Is it useful that mankind spreads out to the stars? I believe so. How would you like the work of Eratosphenes, Tolstoy, Mozart, Einstein, Vangelis, Knopfler to disappear? We need to get out there and add our contribution to the galactic future. The only way we can carry these creations forward, and through freedom, develop them, given our new weapons, is to spread out."

"Well, old Trekker," Maati said. "You have done your bit to help!"

The old man took of his glasses, themselves an antique, and wiped at them with a green cloth, seemingly quite affected.

"The hardest thing to know, before you achieve something great, is to know whether you will achieve it or you are deluding yourself. This does not stop people from working toward their dreams, and I don't think it will stop the human race either. Now Dork, you once wrote a paper about interstellar travel."
"Oh that! I regretted it almost straight away! I lost what little scientific reputation I had, was ridiculed and then, later persecuted for it."
"I know all this, but you seem to focus too much on what other unqualified people thought. What do you think? Were you right?"
"I don't know! It's not easily testable, is it."
"Nevertheless, I would like to discuss this paper with you. We can only travel at 1% of the speed of light so it would take us

400 years to travel to the nearest star Proxima. Can you offer a better engine? It may be that we have become too comfortable here. We may need to break out.."

Chapter 34. Maati's father. Homecoming.

Thanks the maker that one of our darling girls came home, as beautiful and head strong as ever, after her terrible experience on Terra, and as an added bonus for me, and my wife Martha, she'd fallen in love with a fellow there, who seemed decent, if frail. For years she'd resisted all the men who thrown themselves at her, despite the intense pressure that is applied to young folk in our colonies, to procreate and increase the population.

I suppose it was because of this culture, that the first night they stayed with us, we gave them a double bed, and plied them with seaweed hoping for a fruitful coupling. We know that the secret to survival has always been the ability to breed faster than the competition. The Romans knew this. The USA before 1970 also succeeded because they were pretty fertile. Civilisations win in the bedroom, not on the battlefield.

Chapter 35. Maati. What's in the bag?

After making love, Dork tip-toed over to the shower, apparently ashamed of what we'd been doing. I had found it difficult to understand his shame at first, and I had been insulted by it, but I had eventually accepted that Terran culture was different. My father later said that on Terra, sex was probably frowned upon because the place was, after all, already crowded and children were probably not welcome. Perhaps also the world government did not like it because inter-personal relations, love, families, undermine their authority. In contrast here, sex was openly encouraged, because children were desperately needed and the emphasis was on protecting the family. Our behaviour was different because our enemies on Terra were so numerous, and we always had the feeling that outside the walls of our space station there was an infinite universe just waiting to be warmed up with people.

While Dork was in the bathroom showering, I noticed a movement in the corner of the room. I was surprised and amused to see that Dork's bag was lifting itself off the floor. I turned the light on, and immediately the bag dropped to the floor. Puzzled I turned the light off again, and the bag began to lift off the floor again and drift towards the door.

I got out of bed, wrapped myself in a towel, and approached the levitating bag in the dark. It was now closing in on the door, and suddenly a thin pencil of blue laser light shot out of the bag aimed at the door control. Something in the bag was attempting to hack the door to open.

Quickly, I grabbed my gun. I suspected it was some sort of homing device planted on us on the Terra

“Stop! Don’t shoot,” said the bag. A muffled metallic voice.
“Well...stop trying to escape then!” I said.

A curious whining sound emanated from the bag, and the laser light disappeared.

“Morley no harm!”
“Morley? Is that you?”
“A237-Morley is in the bag.”

The bag dropped to the ground and I opened it and let the escapee robot out.

“What were you doing in the bag?”
“Vlad will disintegrate me, because I no good. Must hide, then escape.”
“Where were you thinking of escaping to?”
“Terra.”
“Morley! You’re a traitor!”
“Maybe, but Morley’s brother is with the Terra forces.”

Dork came out of the bathroom, wrapped in a towel, looking, as usual, blissfully innocent. Then he saw Morley.

"Morley?" he turned to me "What's he doing here?"
"He's trying to escape. He's scared of disassembly and he says his brother is with the Terra fleet."
"How can a robot have a brother?"
"Morley, who's your brother?"
"J749-Ataxa. PA to Commander Hambling. He's my brother. From the same evolution-line. Communicate long-distance."

I should at this point explain the evolution-line. The brains of both Terra and colonial robots are, or were, not designed or built in the 20th Century sense. They are fast-evolved in a realistic software environment which rewards hard work, problem solving and morality towards humans, this latter condition being a nod at Asimov's 1st law of robotics. The fact that Morley and his brother are from the same evolution line is very unusual, because usually the evolution in each line leads to only one survivor. On the odd occasion there are two or more survivors, they are called "brothers" (yes, logic and software will always be male dominated).

After this revelation we convinced Morley that we would help him in his attempt to reunite with his brother. His childlike belief in what Maati said to him made our hearts bleed, and I think we both decided that we would help him, if we could. After he had switched himself off, we got back into bed slowly, believing that we had gained a spy in the enemy camp. Dork spoke first.

“There must be some way to use this link.”
“Agreed, but we have to do some thinking first, and I for one need some sleep.”

So while we slept, the Terra fleet slowly and methodically surrounded the colonies. They were in no hurry to attack and lose personnel, and our only remaining hope, a small piece of living metal, lay inert and dreaming of his brother, at the foot of our bed. For a while anyway..

Chapter 36. Janov. Cartoon Insight.

I'd been pacing round my room for hours. In an attempt to come up with a good idea. I'd instructed my entertainment system to play me random clips with the theme of "escape" from our film archives. It had played a clip from Obelix & Co., a cartoon film of one of Goscinny and Uderzo's Asterix series. In this clip, two wild boar were being pursued by the hungry Gauls. One of the boars told the other one to trust him and follow him, and just as their pursuers were upon them Obelix's arms spread out greedily to grasp them, the clever boar led the Gauls onto a Roman patrol. Asterix and Obelix's attentions were thus deflected and they escaped.

Immediately I contacted Prof Kudravtsev
"K! I have an idea."

Chapter 37. Maati. AWOL.

The colonies still used Terran time. Eight hours later we woke up, and dressed quickly. Janov rang us soon after, and we had a chat with his hologram. K also joined in the call.

"Good morning, children."
"Is it?" said Dork.
"Yes. We have an idea to pursue. We're going to split the stations up and move into Saturn."
"Risky," I said.
"Yes, it is, but that way we have the tactical advantage."
"Why is it dangerous?" asked Dork."
"There be dragons!" I said theatrically

I then turned to K and said

"Sir! We've found that Morley the robot is in contact with one of General Hambling's PAs."
"What? How so?"
"They are evolution-line brothers."

K's eyes bulged somewhat.

"Is he a spy?"
"No. However, this is a connection we could use."
"Indeed. We need to think how we can exploit this."

K signed off abruptly with a wave of his hand, and we looked inside Dork's bag for Morley. He wasn't there.

"That robot is completely unpredictable," said Dork.
"Alright. Let's keep calm. He can't have got very far."
"Oh no?" said Dork indicating an open ventilation shaft in the roof.

Suddenly, K's hologram was back.

"Anything wrong?" he said.
"Yes." I said rather sheepishly "Morley has pulled a fast one."
"Not good. How long ago?"
"Not sure. He escaped through the ventilation shaft. He may be trying to see his brother in the Terra fleet."
"That's interesting. About an hour back we detected a small object leaving the station, slowly. We thought "debris". Could be your spy."

K turned to his colleague

"Kolya, do you have trajectory of that small piece of debris you found?"

K turned back toward us.

"It does look like your robot. Less than a metre in size, travelling towards the flag ship of the Terra fleet, speed about 0.5 metres per second. They're stationed at 9 km away so at that rate he will have covered 20% of the distance."

Think you two could catch him in your ship?"

"Yes. We're on our way. Send the trajectory data to the Little Cow."

Chapter 38. Dork. Little Cow.

The Little Cow was her ship. Maati was obviously pleased to see it again. She told me that it was called Little Cow, because it steered as badly as one and all the boys had called her that, so she's took it as her honorary name. In case you were wondering: the Amish had cows. The ship was spherical and was pushed by a high-performance ion engine.

I was hustled into the passenger seat. The doors in front of us opened and we slowly pulled out into space. I had a sudden feeling of vertigo, as 50 miles or so beneath us, wrapped in shades of cracked white and blue was Enceladus, which like Terra was mostly covered in ice. Vast plumes of water were rising up from the south pole, and you could see the plumes slowly twist and join, and feed, Saturn's rings. A beautiful rainbow could also been seen as the distant Sun caught it. We began to accelerate upwards away from Enceladus, following Morley's path.

"That's where we get our water and chemicals."
"What a sight!"
"I've picked up dear old Morley on the radar."
"How long till we get there?"
"Ten minutes. Damn, I've picked up some Terran ships beyond him."
"What?"
"Just means we'll have to get in and out quick."

"Maybe we should go back," I said, trying to sound persuasive.

Maati looked across at me amused.

"If you're worried about your safety, don't be. I prefer it out here to following our comrades into Saturn."
"What's in Saturn?"
"Sprites"
"Sprites?"
"Yes, electric vampires the size of a ship. They hover there in the helium atmosphere in areas where the gas is moving upwards, powered by the lightning that occurs there. So long as you avoid the up draughts, you're OK."

I looked at her very closely to see if she was joking. She had tricked me before, telling me that there were rats on the space station. A trick that had caused me to demolish several small and innocent cleaning robots.

"There," she shouted suddenly. I followed her finger out into space, past the Enceladan snow and far in the distance was a blinking light, Morley, patiently drifting towards the Terra fleet.
"Now. This is where you come in, my love. I want you to grab Morley with the robot arm as I fly past."
"Good, I was beginning to think I was just the light relief."
"If you were, you'd be doing a lousy job. See that glove in front of you? Put your hand in. See? The arm has extended. Just move your arms as normal and the artificial arm will mimic whatever you do."

What fun it was. I tried a few trial poses. I raised a finger at the enemy.

"Alright. We are about to pass him by. Ready?"
"Aye Cap'n."

I wished I'd been sporty as a youth. I had tried to avoid games as much as possible, so my catching skill was an embarrassment. Nevertheless, I caught Morley first time. He didn't struggle. He had probably switched himself off, in fact. Maati, busy at the controls, preparing to turn us round, smiled at me.

"Well done! Now let's get home, fast!"

But Mars the God of war was watching, and we were suddenly hit by a projectile weapon, and blue sparks began to fly in the cabin.

"I may be a bit naïve, but it seems we've been hit," I said, facetiously.
"Is this your attempt at light relief?"

Maati was struggling with the controls.

"Damn. We've lost thrust. Dork, throw Morley at our space station will you?"
"Excuse me?"

"Just throw him towards our space station! I'll radio them and they'll pick him up. The enemy won't be able to detect Morley."

My heart sank.

"Does that mean we'll be captured?"
"Maybe. We've lost power. But don't worry. I'm sure we can escape again."
"Optimistic aren't you?"
"Once you've escaped from Terra, you tend to be."

So, I threw the still comatose Morley towards our space station as best I could. I was probably a radian away from the correct direction, but I supposed the colonists would be out looking for him. Maati contacted them and told them what had happened and asked them to intercept Morley. Then, once again we were left looking at each other.

"What now?" I said in trepidation.
"We could play cards till they arrive. Do you know blackjack?"
"No."
"Shame."
"We could have some fun. Know sex?"
"No."
"Shame."

Maati's face lit up.

"You're obsessed with me, aren't you?"

And so it was that half an hour later, we were in a state of extreme satisfaction and calm, but still drifting.

Chapter 39. Gen Hambling. Into Saturn.

It was during the fourth day of our seige, that the colonist's space station began splitting up, into individual ships which then began, one by one, to plunge into Saturn's atmosphere. I called a conference, of course. Guiy, cursing under his breath, recommended that we wait for their reappearance.

"They can't stay in there for more than a few days with all the electric storms."

However, I wasn't convinced. It was perfectly possible that they could stay submerged for week, this was their environment, and my superiors back on Terra were eager and impatient for a quick victory, as rebellions sympathetic to the colonists had broken out in Indonesia and Africa.

Therefore I ordered half of our fleet, 20 ships, to follow the colonists as best they could. Inside a gas cloud, which is what Saturn effectively is, the visibility was a disaster, but sound travels effectively in a gas, and tracking of the colonists was possible using sonar.

Chapter 40. Ensign Dan Rustn. There Be Dragons!

Four days after arriving at Saturn, our ship, the UNS Potomac, dove with the rest of the fleet into its atmosphere. What a mistake that was! My colleagues and I were all well trained to cope with stress, and of course we carried on with our duties as we had hitherto, but as we plunged into the deeper layers of the gas giant even the toughest of us lost morale. The view screens showed little. The gas looked just like free space. Ollie, sitting next to me on the acoustic monitoring equipment heard the sound first.

"What the gazump is the moaning?" he said, staring straight ahead into nothing and holding his headphones.
"It's your imagination. I didn't know you had such a dirty mind."

He grimaced, rolled his eyes, and rocked his head from side to side as if he was trying to lose his ears.

"It's not imaginary. Listen! It sounds like a dirty phone call."

He handed the headphones to me, which I wasn't so pleased about since he's an unhygienic bugger.

"OK. I can hear it. It sounds like whale song."
"Whale? What the hell is a whale?"

Some people just don't know anything do they?

“Where we you when the rest of us were in school? It was a mammal big as a ship which looked like a bleeding fish, extinct since the Big Shift…”
“Well, whatever a whale is, that one needs a psychiatrist.”
“Seems to be coming from all over.”
“OK. A cetacean asylum then.”
“It’s getting louder. Any visual contact?”
“Nothing distinct. A few ghostly shapes below us.”
“Any movement?”
“Nothing on the scopes.”

I contacted our duty officer, commander Rogerson, straight away and reported it. He breezed in, hot from the gym, radiating good health and confidence.

“You say we have something like a whale below us?”
“Yessir. Approaching slowly, contact in 5 minutes.”
“I guess we should tell Captain Ahab he was looking in the wrong ocean!”

We were all a bit bemused by this one: Cmdr Rogerson never makes much sense to us. Then my heart froze as I saw on the viewscreen one of the whales change course, right towards us. I may not know who this Captain Ahab was, but I can sure recognise a living thing when I see one. I wasn’t the only one who saw the move either, because Cmdr Rogerson immediately sounded general stations, and the emergency red lights came on. This didn’t do anything for our state of mind, since we had no idea what this enemy was. All eyes were on the view screen which was dark, but for the occasional flash of lightning.

It happened so fast. On the view screen the diffuse shape, like an electric squid, seemed to leap at us faster than we had thought possible. I'm no Prof, but the thing was obviously not composed of the usual heavy stuff. Then it surrounded us, and for want of a better phrase, we began to die. It wasn't your usual quick end, but a gradual fading of the senses which is hard to describe. As the ship's lights died, and the view screen dimmed, I found it hard to move my arms and even my eyes. My sight and hearing dimmed, and most peculiar of all, my mind became peaceful like never before.

Of course, we all know now that these so called sprites eat electrons, the units of electricity, so that any electrical circuit, including some of those in the extremities of the human body, are damped. Luckily they don't harm the body's inner functions, water protects them from the electromagnetic effects.

As you can tell, since I'm writing this little spiel, we were saved, though most of us didn't notice for several hours. Our kind saviours were several flashes of lightning that erupted in our vicinity and drew off the sprites. An almost paralysed Cmdr Rogerson somehow managed to convince the ship to reroute back out into free space. Our orders could go hang.

Chapter 41. Maati. An Insight.

We'd been sitting around in the slowly rotating ship for an age when Dork gazing out of the window suddenly broke the silence.

"I spy with my little eye, something beginning with S."
"Star! Now will you shut up?"

It was at this moment that there was a metallic bang on the side of the ship. We both looked at each other in alarm. Had we been grabbed by a Terran ship? Scrapings and thuds then began above us, slowly moving down towards the front of the ship. Dork looked at me in alarm.

"Do you have scavengers in deep space?"
"There are some pirates out by Jupiter way, groups of extreme Mormons & one group who based their constitution of Star Trek, but..."
"One of your dragons?"
"It sounds like a maintenance robot."

We both realised who it was simultaneously.

"Morley!" we said to each other.

The scraping suddenly stopped and the beautiful sight, under the circumstances, of Morley appeared at the window. At the same time all the computer systems began to come back on.

"I don't know how he did it, but he did it. Let's let him in."

Morley entered the airlock, and was already in full flow when we let him into the cabin.

"Morley repair ship yes? All forgiven yes?"
"Morley you are a little genius!"
"Morley agree."

Dork, having literally thrown Morley back towards the colony was puzzled by his sudden appearance.

"Morley! How did you even get back here? The last we knew you were on your way to the station sleeping soundly!"
"Morley used micro-engine. Very slow, but Morley turned round."

We weren't entirely out of the woods yet though. I knew that Morley had attached the spare battery to the ship's circuitry, but that would not be enough to drive the ion engine. We'd have to use the solar sail.

"OK, chaps. Looks like the Little Cow is going photon sailing!"
"Won't it take ages?"
"Yes, but it's better than sitting here twiddling our thumbs, isn't it!"
"If you say so..."

"Morley likes sailing."
"Watch this Dork. It's always a beautiful sight."

Unfortunately, the Solar sail didn't deploy.

"Isn't something supposed to be moving?"
"Yes, dammit."
"So, no wings.."
"Well, yes, unless – Morley, can you go out and have look."

Morley in his haste to please smashed himself into the airlock door and tottered around the spacecraft in daze, and got tangled up in a floating seat belt.

"Morley, you have to open doors before you go through them."
"Morley forget."

We unwound Morley from the seatbelt and ejected him bursting with pride out of the airlock. He radioed back a few minutes later with his diagnosis that the solar sail connectors had been partially melted in the blast we had sustained, and it would take a bit of pulling to free them, more pulling than Morley could provide, and more than I could provide. I looked at Dork, his build didn't bear out much hope either.

"Sorry Dork. Looks like we'll both have to go out and give it a pull."
"Go out? You mean, out there?"
"What else could 'out' mean? Come on, it's only a vacuum."

Dork tilted his head very peculiarly at this.

“What did you say?”
“Only a vacuum”.
“That’s it!”
“Are you having an aneurysm?”

Chapter 42, Dork. Horizon Drive to the Rescue.

The age old problem that had kept mankind form even considering interstellar flight was fuel. The nearest star system to us is Proxima Centauri, which is about four light years away. In order to get there in a human lifetime and without having to try and freeze people, you have to travel at a fairly large fraction of the speed of light to do it, say 10 percent of that speed. If you're using rockets then to get up to that speed you need a lot of fuel. How much? As much as, probably, the mass of Enceladus. This is obviously ludicrous from an engineering point of view. But, the invention of thrust from the vacuum by theorists before the Crustal Shift and by a few people on the fringe such as me and K was that fuel or propellant is not needed. If you can make a spaceship move simply by damping the vacuum (the zero point field) on one side of it, then you'll have acceleration without fuel.

In other words, the colonists didn't have to mess around in Saturn. Why not go to Proxima or Alpha Centauri? I told Maati and Morley. Maati simply said that I was starting to sound like Prof K, and Morley jumped up with the shock of revelation and banged himself on the ceiling in surprise.

Not only that, but we could apply this to our own situation. The zero point field is like an invisible wavy ocean that surrounds everything uniformly so the overall force is zero. A window on Terra is subject to massive atmospheric pressure from both directions. The window sits there intact, and all this force is invisible, because the forces cancel. It was well known from the Casimir effect that two close parallel plates damp this quantum 'sea' between themselves to such a degree that it produces a force pushing the plates together, and the plates have that effect when they are about 10 nm apart, so if we can damp waves of that sort of shortness on one side of the craft then we'd move that way. Why not just make an antennae on the side of the station of fractal nature so it damps the zero point waves as they pass creating a damped zone? The darker area on the drawing below. Then we would slowly drift towards that damped zone. No need for fuel.

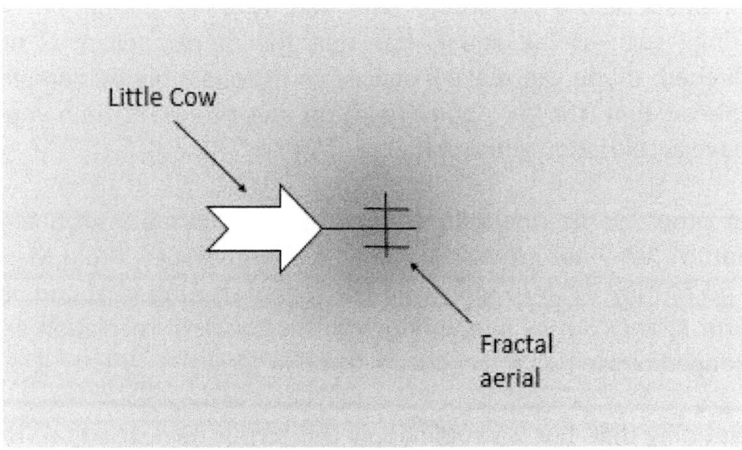

Morley understood the idea right away and set to work. He ripped apart a non-essential radio system and used his internal

3d printer to make a few fractal antennas. I worked out the frequency we needed, which depended on our desired acceleration. Morley attached it to the outside of the craft and we switched it on.

"I don't feel any acceleration," said Maati, rolling her eyes slowly.
"Give it time. It's cumulative. It builds up slowly."
"Like you."
"Why, thank you!"

I spent the time designing a similar system for the modules of the colonists, while Maati helped Morley to repair himself with other 3d printed parts.

Chapter 43, Yoder. The First Sub-Aether Message.

We could not stay inside Saturn forever, the "chaff" we sent out to draw off the Sprites would last a few days, then we'd have to come out fighting. The whole colony was in a mood of desperation. Families were saying good bye to each other. People spoke in muted tones without energy. It was clear morale was low. It was my fault. I'd dragged them in here, simply because I could not think of a better solution.

I was alone on the bridge of the Gustloss. My family: wife and five kids, were on a civilian craft but I was unable to communicate with them. Radio waves cannot penetrate Saturn's highly-charged atmosphere, but we were working on a method of communication using sound waves, which do travel well in gas.

Some signals were now coming in by this method and I was monitoring them. It was not cheering me up because most of the messages were complaining about the idiocy of coming into Saturn in the first place.

Some of them however were mentioning a problem with the communication and in my experience, problems are opportunities for discovery. There was a random signal interfering with the communication. The external microphones were picking up a random set of pulses that sometimes drowned out the transmissions. The conclusions was that it was the Sprites" communication – Saturnian whale song. Other ships then came on the line. The signals did not seem to be exactly random.

As you might have guessed from my name or the number of my children, I am Amish, but I left the faith after the age of 30 (and five kids) and went into, of all things military cryptography. So I ran the spurious signal through all the algorithms in the book. Nothing. Becker-Hornstein? No. Chen-Wright? Mazovski Plume? No. This was taking forever, but I had nothing else to do. A somewhat desperate party was going on down the corridor and I could hear the simging. Feeling rather in the need for a little music myself I plugged the signal into the loudspeakers, and then I knew.

Morse code!

In these days of high tech, there's never a piece of paper or a pencil around when you need one so I typed it on the screen.

Z, V, O

Damn. Gibberish!

U, S, 0, N.

3, 0, E, 6, 2, K

No, gibberish. At times like these one clutches at anything. I grabbed the whiskey by my side and was about to down it, when I noticed it had a map of Scotland on it with north and east co-ordinates. I made the connection immediately. Who says truth is not found in the bottle? Suddenly I was back in business. With another scan through the repeated message it said.

"Dork has tech for escape to Proxima. Pls rendezvous 0N, 30E, 62k altitude, Sunday AM. I & D."

I guessed that I & D was Maati and Dork but where were they, and how were they broadcasting this acoustic message? In fact, were they broadcasting the message at all? What if this was a Terran ruse? Why is nothing easy?

Chapter 44. A Random Sprite. Outsiders!

For millennia we had been safe in our world. All sounds in it accounted for and understood. This new signal was unnerving for it seemed to contain information but we could not decode it. Even thinking-together we could not do it. In our experience, object were either inert from outside: just asteroids burning up, or warm and information-ful like our comrades. These signal looked information-ful but were not. Some panicked and ran to the other side of the world. Some of us, a very few, were curious and came closer.

The food that they provided was good, probably as a peace offering. It was appreciated and so we left them alone.

Chapter 45. Dork. Sub-Aether.

"Well, according to the quasar navigation, we are in position. I hope they got my message."
"There's no reply yet. Do they know how to reply to your inertial stuff?"
"K should work it out."

As you may have guessed I'd used the quantum vacuum to communicate with them. Morley and I had found that we could use a doughnut-shaped double-plate to make voids in the quantum vacuum that propagated away. We'd been trying to rig a better transmitter and Morley has been jerking around a little more than he usually is. Eventually I realised that quantum voids were propagating out from the doughnut and altering his inertial mass. We immediately began transmitting Morse code at Saturn. The first communication by what you might call sub-aether. Of course, the signal was going to be extremely small given the power we had available but the idea was that this was a fundamental channel that no one else could monitor and it should show up in acoustics, since sound waves are pressure waves and if you modify inertia, you also modify pressure.

Also, what is not really well understood about this modification of inertia is how powerful it really is. If you modify the inertia of an object from the quantum background with the same amount of input power, and then do it again with a more massive object then the percentage change in inertia will be the same. This is because you are modifying a background field, giving a very fundamental field a gradient, so that whatever mass you have, no matter how many atoms it contains, each atom will fall down that gradient at a given acceleration. So the force is independent of the mass.

Chapter 46. Maati. Morley the Hero.

We'd been waiting there for hours it seemed. Waiting for any sign that they had heard us. I had believed in Dork's new method of communication. After all, the horizon drive had worked very well. I must admit I began to criticise him a little out of frustration. We were in mid-argument when suddenly we both noticed an emphatic metallic bang on the outside of the hull.

"Not good." I said.

We both rushed to the window to see a cable taught and attached to a Terran ship. We started to accelerate. We then heard a quick voice behind us

"Morley fix!"

And as we turned, we heard Morley slam into the airlock and air-gas himself out into space. I screamed after him, but, as Dork said, those kind of sound waves do not travel in the vacuum. We could hear him rolling over the hull using his magnetic wheels and cutting through the cable with his laser. I was banging on the window like a lunatic so Dork had to drag me away in case I cracked the glass.

Chapter 47. Dork. Contact.

Yeah, Maati went crazy! I'd never seen her like that. I tried to drag her away from the window as she was completely unhinged. I had not realised she was so attached to Morley, but she was too strong for me and kept watching. When he disengaged the cable he pushed off with it in the direction of the Terra ship and gave us momentum in the opposite direction via Newton's third law.

She was making so much noise and crying, that at first I did not recognise the radio was blurting out a message.

"Maati and Dork. Come in!"

Maati was in no state to speak, so I answered was so relieved to hear Yoder.

"Hello. We're at the rendezvous. Where are you?"
"Look out of your window. Towards Saturn."

The colonists ship was beneath us, skimming along the Saturnian cloud tops, leaving a von Karman street in their wake. Odd how, even in the midst of anguish, beautiful phenomena can occur.

"OK, kid. Watch the show."

Even as he said that, the Terra ship, and another that had been hiding behind them, opened fire on Yoder's ship. Immediately from out of the gas cloud of Saturn there erupted what looked like an electrified ghost. Dragging gas behind it, it surged up and engulfed the Terra ship whose lights immediately went out.

Our lights flickered as well, but only slightly. I clapped, despite myself, and congratulated the colonists on a trap well set. Maati had rallied by this time and was trying to contact Morley on the radio. Only static came back – perhaps not surprisingly as an electromagnetic phenomenon was occurring in the vicinity.

Chapter 48. Yoder. How to Get to Proxima Centauri.

We managed to get the Little Cow into our hold quickly. Maati was in a state, still trying to contact Morley. Quick thinking and action was essential now so I quizzed Dork on his text. The details of the method of propulsion seems quite simple, so we broadcast them, acoustically, round the fleet. We got K into the debate by phone and he came up with three problems with Dork's suggestion of fleeing to Proxima.

1) The acceleration would be low so we'd still have to fight the Terrans off for some time.
2) What happens in deep space when we end up at 10% of the speed of light and small grains of interstellar dust pack the same punch as getting hit by an asteroid?
3) Are we sure that Proxima has water?

Dork's answers sounded completely crazy to me, but I passed them on.

1) He proposed a new weapon called an inertial shield that apparently was able to alter the inertial mass of missiles and push them off course.
2) He suggested pushing an asteroid in front of us for the interstellar dust.
3) Evidence for water on Proxima has been found just before the Big Shift. As part of his work on Terra he had had access to these records.

We put these to K.

"Your answers are reasonable but you are not familiar with our environment out here. There is another solution. Instead of an asteroid we can push water in front of us. That will help us survive and also shield us from any particles we might encounter."
"An asteroid sized blob of water. I suppose it might hold together gravitationally but where do we get that much water?"
"From Enceladus. Do you know how much water that moon throws out into space every day?"
"OK. But how are we going to collect it? With buckets?"
"We have tugs designed just for that."

Images of their take-off from Terra were plaguing Dork for some reason. Images of missiles approaching their craft. Missiles that suddenly and rather comically were brushed aside by the inertial field around the craft.

"That's it! All we have to do is make the inertial mass of approaching space dust greater to the front of the leading craft. That will act as an inertial lens and deflect any solid objects away to the side."

Here's a schematic showing this:

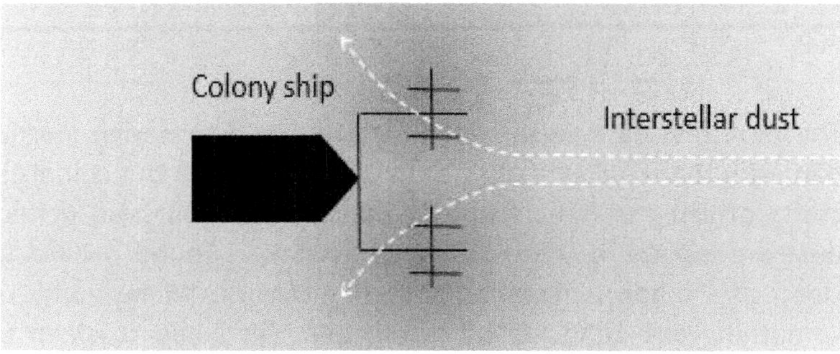

"How?"
"You make sure the areas of damped vacuum are in front the ship, of course, to drag it forward, but also you split them so that there are two slightly to the side producing an area of higher vacuum just in front of the ship, to push the incoming interstellar dust aside. Has to be designed just right."

K was suddenly filled with decisions.

"That's it! OK, now we have to work out how to do it, while we have time."

Maati then spoke up.

"How about we negotiate, to gain time?"
"OK. I'll have my staff start that process, but they may not believe we mean it without someone going out there to negotiate in person."

Chapter 49. Dork. Working the Details.

The next few days were hectic for me. I had to design inertial dampers that could be built onto the front of all the colonists' crafts of just the right shape to pull the craft but also deflect dust around them. With so much at stake I found it hard to sleep. If I made I mistake? If it didn't work, I'd be guilty of something like genocide by negligence, yet I had to sleep to maintain my reason. I failed to solve that problem so I had to consume vast quantities of coffee and triple check everything. Morley also checked my work for errors in logic.

On the second day K came to see me, looking old and frail. Maybe he had had a similar couple of days. He sat down next to my desk in my only sofa with a grunt, saying.

"I wish we'd had more time to talk. I liked your papers."
"I wish I'd come out here sooner, but you know. I was comfortable."
"I want you to replace me as Chief Scientist."
"Why? Are you going somewhere?"

He paused a little, then said

"No, but I'm getting old. My mind is not as clear as it was. We need to be sharp now that we're going," he indicated the window, "out there!"
"Well, OK."

"Good!"

He said, getting up. The last thing he said, with a break in his voice was

"Look after them! Get them safely away."

If it had not been for lack of sleep I might have said a little more and realised his meaning, but I simply promised I would, and then went back to work immediately, designing the inertial deflector. It had to be built from materials we had to hand. It was mostly composed of metal plates and of course worked in a similar manner to the Casimir effect. The only difference was that it was asymmetric and the vacuum had to be energised to enhance the effect. I emailed the designs to all the other ships and they immediately began making the modifications, still amid the safety of Saturn's atmosphere.

Then Maati came blasting into the room, with Morley of course.

"K's gone!"
"Gone where?"
"We don't know, but he was mumbling about someone called Hess and I looked him up - I think he's flown over to try to negotiate peace."

Suddenly our conversation made sense, and I said, somewhat callously.

"He's sacrificing himself."

Maati hit me on the arm, and with tears in her eyes she stormed out of the room. Morley stayed behind.

"Maati has malfunction?"
"No. Morley, she's actually working well. She is female after all."
"Morley does not understand."
"Perhaps for the best. If you did, you might become as crazy as us!"

Maati stormed back in.

"Morley, how can I storm out, if you don't come with me!"

Morley looked at me and then stormed out with Maati.

Chapter 50. Kudravtsev. In Captivity.

As probably to be expected, when I had sailed across to see the Terrans they had not listened very well. They had beaten me badly, despite my age, and asked the wrong questions. I'd not answered, so they tied me up in a cell and forgot about me. I was quite prepared to die, but I did want to know what was happening outside. After some time I heard electromagnetic cannons firing and crew-members running in the corridors outside, but there was no news.

Then after a few hours the door opened, but no-one came in. I immediately assumed that they'd decided to terminate me and I ran through the prayers I had prepared. Then a robot came through the door.

"Morley! How did you get here?"
"Not Morley. His brother."

He looked the same, but he had had far fewer knocks by the look of him.

"Ok. Then, I'll call you Horley."
"Name accepted," he said stiffly.
"Boy. We'd better loosen you up before you meet Morley."

Chapter 51. Hambling. The Showdown.

I could tell that Cmdr Guiy was relishing every moment as Kudravsev was brought to the bridge in a wheelchair. Kudravtsev was in a bad way. Had been beaten, and for an old man, looked just about done. His white hair was flecked with red.

"Well, well, the Trekker himself," said Guiy. "We meet again at last." He indicated that Kudravtsev should be woken up. A soldier hit him on the head.

"Good morning Guiy," he said, somewhat slurred.
"Not for you," said Guiy. "I'm here to watch you squirm as your colonists are nuked."
"You never did follow the law," said K.
"No law out here. Terran law stops at the edge of the atmosphere."
"How convenient."
"Isn't it? Fire the first missile."
"Wait!"
"I know what you're trying to do. Delay me? Why is it that villains in Hollywood movies always wait, allowing a counter-strike? Not this time!"

At this point I intervened.

"Sir, I have to tell you that if you use that weapon it'll be

genocide."
"Hambling, I'm aware of your treasonous thoughts. Guards, seize him."

I was set upon by two of his political officers and parked face down on the floor.

Guiy looked at Kudravtsev in satisfaction and said, savouring every syllable.

"Fire!"

Everyone on the bridge watched the missile approaching the largest of the colonists' ships. They had all been slowly accelerating away towards the edge of the Solar system, but we had been keeping pace with them. Kudravtsev, I noticed, crossed his fingers behind his back. Oddly, there was a robot under his wheelchair.

The explosion was massive. I could see it from the floor and the entire ship rocked shortly after. The technicians were a little surprised to see such a large explosion and there was a certain amount of chatter.

"Quiet! What are you all chattering about?"

One of the technicians, a little bolder than the others said

"Well, Sir, the explosion was rather larger than we expected."

"Quite right. Soon we will be one global government again."

Kudravtsev head was bowed. Guiy was pacing up and down.

"Well? Any signs of survivors. We carry ten other missiles."
"Er, .. Yes Sir."
"How many?"
"All of them, Sir!"
"What?"

Kudravtsev looked up quickly. Guiy went to him immediately, cuffed him across the head.

"What is this? What defence do they have?"
"It's called inertial damping."
"What?"
"You see the glass keeping the air in this ship?"
"Yes, so?"
"It has to be strong to resist the air pressure pushing out right?"
"I don't want a lesson in physics."
"You're going to get one. Your last lesson. There's something else apart from the air that exerts pressure – the zero point field. It's everywhere, pushing on us from all directions. Normally we don't notice it because its effects cancel out, but what if you were to damp it in one particular area?"
"Well what?"
"Then things would be pushed by the zero point field into that area."
"What is this rubbish?"

"As a perfectly random example, you might drag the energy from a nuclear blast into that area, thus defusing it."
"I see.."
"You might also drag the body of a particularly annoying human into one area too."
"Rubbish, the zero point field is pseudoscience and you're a quack."
"What a shame. If you hadn't banned the tech, you'd be way ahead."
"This is a ruse – they must have some other method."
"You want proof? OK, then."

Cmdr Guiy then exhaled, and held his head. He started speaking, but his words came out shrill.

"What are you doing? What's happening to me?"
"Just an empirical demonstration," said Kudravtsev. "You always needed a shrink."

Guiy sank to his knees, obviously in agony, but we could see nothing wrong with him, until blood started appearing from cracks in his body. I won't describe what happened then as his body was slowly sucked down to about the size of a tennis ball, and then slowly dissipated like smoke. The staff on the bridge, even his thuggish guards, looked on in horror – not knowing what to do. It was unclear where the attack was coming from, but I signalled to those of my men who I knew were bold and loyal and they took advantage of the chaos to shoot Guiy's men and regain control of the bridge. I slowly walked up to

Kudravtsev.

"I hope you are not going to do that again."

My mouth was dry.

"No, I'm done. I hope you are a different sort of person."
"I am."
"Let my people go?"

There was no doubt in my mind. They'd behaved honourably towards me in the Battle above Terra, and we'd behaved terribly towards them.

"Sure, Moses. I hope you realise that not all Terran people are like that."
"I hope you realise we colonists do not always stoop to violence either."
"I know so."
"Good, then."
"Oh. When you get to Proxima Centauri, ..give us a call. OK?"

Chapter 52. Dork. Interstellar Trek.

The Sun was now an even-more distant speck. We were at a distance of 200 AU and still accelerating up towards 10% of the speed of light. The horizon drives were working well, and the "Cowcatchers", as we had christened the inertial shields, were doing a good job of deflecting particles away so far and everyone was looking forward to seeing Proxima in about four years.

Kudravtsev had been returned to us by the Terrans with words of goodwill, and Morley of course had survived and returned, so Maati was in a good mood again. So much so that the nights were warm and I was quite looking forward to being confined inside a ship for four years.

We were looking at Proxima Centauri through a telescope. It still looked tiny, but it was to be our new home. We knew, from data collected before the Big Shift that it had water oceans. I couldn't wait to see it.

Maati, playing cards with Morley and his brother, Horley, seemed keen to be off to bed. The robots, in between playing, were building a third robot. Their 'son', to be named Norley.

"So, fella," she said. "You coming to bed?"
"Why the sudden hurry? Are these two guys beating you hollow?"

"Yes, but that's not the reason."
"What then?"
"I'm just remembering something my sister once said."
"What was that?"
"I'll tell you someday. Something about children, exponential growth & the limitless future."
"I didn't know your sister was so smart."
"Very. Come on."

**** THE END ****